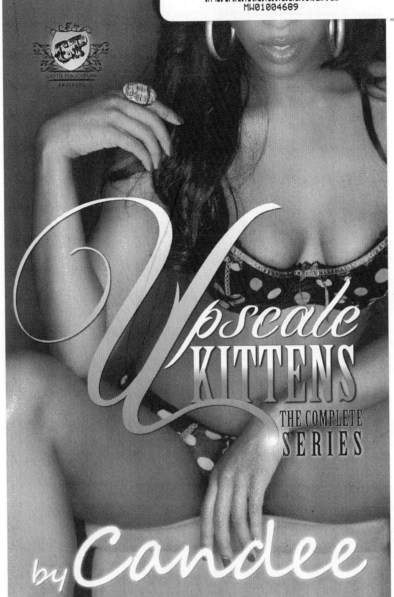

Upscale
KITTENS
THE COMPLETE
SERIES

by Candee

PUBLISHER'S NOTE:
This book is a work of fiction. Names, characters, businesses, Organizations, places, events and incidents are the product of the Author's imagination or are used fictionally. Any resemblance of Actual persons, living or dead, events, or locales are entirely coincidental.

Library of Congress Control Number: 2013936709
ISBN 10: 0984303057

ISBN 13: 978-0984303052

Cover Design: Davida Baldwin www.oddballdsgn.com
Editor: Advanced Editorial Services
Graphics: Davida Baldwin
www.thecartelpublications.com
First Edition

Printed in the United States of America

CHECK OUT OTHER TITLES BY THE CARTEL PUBLICATIONS

Dedication

This novel is dedicated to all the Cartel Publications
fans everywhere! We love you all!

What's Poppin' Fam,

I am so excited right now. As I am drafting this letter to you, I have just completed and uploaded my first novel. My book is called, "Hersband Material" and it's available now. This was a long time coming for me, and I'm boosted that it's finally done. So make sure you check it out.

Now to the present book, "Upscale Kittens", Candee did an excellent job of weaving a good tale together. This story of love, sibling rivalry, domestic abuse, drug abuse and revenge is amazing. You will be pleased.

Keeping in line with tradition, we want to give respect to a trailblazer paving the way. With that said we want to recognize:

Tina Smith-Brown

Tina Smith-Brown is the author of the break out novel, "Fish & Grits". If you want to read a phenomenal book that takes you from your world and pulls you into another one, a book so fantastic you never want it to end, you must read this!

Aight, get to it! I'll see you in the next novel. ;)

Be Easy!
Charisse "C. Wash" Washington
Vice President

The Cartel Publications
www.thecartelpublications.com
www.twitter.com/cartelbooks
www.facebook.com/cartelpublications

Prologue

Jazzy eyed her sister Angela's horrified expression, as she pushed her into the basement along with her two younger sisters, Nandi and Love. A loud banging noise at the front door upstairs signified what was about to happen, someone was going to die.

Standing in front of a large white deep freezer, Angela stooped down and addressed her three sisters. "Listen, I know ya'll don't understand what's happening right now," she whispered, wiping the flowing tears from her chubby cheeks, "but ya'll gotta stay down here and hide. And no matter what you hear, you can't go back upstairs." Her pregnant belly rubbed against fifteen-year-old Jazzy's arm, who was standing closest to her.

"What's going on," Jazzy sobbed quietly, grabbing Angela's sweaty hand. "Why Mr. Berger threatening to hurt you? Why he acting mean? We did everything he said didn't we?"

"Don't worry about all that," Angela said yanking her arm. "The less you know the better." The sound of the wooden front door cracking upstairs startled her. "He's in here, ya'll gotta get inside this freezer and don't get out! I'm not fucking around with ya'll."

"No, Angie," ten-year-old Nandi sniveled, "I don't wanna get on mommy." She looked at the freezer and her body trembled. "I'm scared."

"You gotta do it," Angela responded gripping her sister's elbow roughly, periodically looking up at the stairs. "I'm sorry, but I don't want him to hurt you guys. Please do this for me. I'm begging you."

Angela never wanted this for her sisters. She knew that going into the icy freezer, where their mother lay frozen dead, would traumatize them. Unfortunately it was the only place they could hide, because the man they all feared was smart enough to check every other inch of the house for them. He would never in a million years think they would be crazy enough to hide there, but he was wrong.

"Angela," the maniac screamed from upstairs. "Where are you?"

Angela grabbed the thick gray moving pad off the floor, and opened the large white freezer. A blast of fog crawled out, and pillowed the air above their heads. She threw it inside and spread it over her mother's frozen corpse. When she was done she lifted Nandi's thin body off of the floor, and placed her inside kicking and screaming. Nandi clasped for Angela's arms in and effort to pull herself back out, but she was no match for her older sister's strength, or love.

When Nandi was safe she turned to her other sister. "Get inside, Jazzy and Love."

Thirteen-year-old Love hopped inside without another word, and positioned herself on top of the blanket. She lost feelings for her mother a long time ago, and wanted only to save her and her sisters' lives. The coolness of the air, and the stiffness of her mother's body, immediately sent chills up her spine.

"Don't let Nandi get out," Angela said to Jazzy and Love, "no matter what."

Jazzy hopped inside of the freezer, and pulled Nandi toward her warm body. The moment Jazzy was inside, his footsteps moving across the floor indicated he was rushing toward the basement.

"He's coming," Angela said frantically. She removed her shoe and white sock. "Keep this sock stuffed on the corner so air can get inside, and the lid of the freezer won't close all the way." She kissed her finger, and touched each of them over their tiny lips. "Remember me, and remember I always loved you. And, Jazzy, you gotta make sure ya'll always stay together, even if you got to run away to do it. Let nobody pull you apart." She slowly closed the freezer's door, hiding her sisters inside.

"What the fuck are you doing down here?" Cyrus Berger, a DC Police Officer, asked Angela.

"Nothing...uh...what do you want?"

"Is it true? Are you pregnant with my baby? When you know I got a wife and kid at home already? Huh? I mean what type of shit is this, Angela? I thought we had an understanding. And here you are trying to trap a nigga."

While Angela tried to diffuse the situation brewing outside, inside of the dark freezer things were heating up when Nandi had lost her mind. "Jazzy, I don't want to be on mama's face," Nandi whispered inside the freezer. "I'm scared."

Jazzy, who was afraid Cyrus would hear Nandi's voice, placed her hand over her mouth and squeezed tightly, silencing her immediately.

Outside of the freezer things weren't any better. "Yes it's your baby, Cyrus, but you don't have nothing to worry about," Angela told him. "I swear I'm going to do right by this child on my own. I'm not coming to you for child support or nothing like that. It ain't even about that with me, you know that."

"But, you lied to me," Cyrus yelled. "You fucking lied to me, you fucking fat bitch! You threw that pussy at me knowing I was weak, and now you trying to trap me. For months I been coming over here, and asking you about your weight gain. And there you were, telling me lies, and saying that you were just getting big. And now I'm hearing that you got my kid. I'm sorry, Angela, but I can't let you keep it. I just can't." He paused for a second, and looked around. "Where are your sisters?"

"They not here—"

"Then where the fuck are they," he screamed cutting her off.

"I let them...um...they went to play over their friend's. You know the girl who sells the ice cream cones out of her house up the block. They are there."

"What's the address?"

"Cyrus, please, they are my sisters. And they don't know anything."

"Well I can't feel safe with that answer. Now what is the address that they are at?"

"They are just babies, Cyrus," Angela giggled trying to relax his mind, "you don't have to worry about them saying nothing to anybody. They are smart and know better. Half of the time they don't even know what's going on around here anyway. I promise you everything will be fine. With me, this baby, and my sisters. Your secret is safe with me."

"I know," he said before raising his gun to her forehead, and pulling the trigger. "I'm going to make sure of that."

POP. POP. POP.

Angela's body made a loud thud as it fell onto the concrete basement floor.

"A....la," Nandi screamed through Jazzy's muffled fingers, trying to say Angela's name.

Jazzy pressed her hand against Nandi's lips so hard, she could feel Nandi's warm blood ooze between her fingers, from her teeth gashing into the flesh of her hand.

Cyrus grabbed his radio from his chest and said, "I need backup at 5692 Martin Luther King Jr. Blvd, I just found the Law woman in the freezer. Her oldest daughter tried to stab me when I discovered the woman's frozen corpse."

Jazzy's heart beat heavily in her chest, not only because Cyrus just murdered her sister, but also because he was pretending as if he knew nothing about her mother, or her death. Of course he knew Shannon Law was inside that freezer, it was his idea, and he placed her there with Angela's help.

Upscale KITTENS

When she overdosed from heroin about two years earlier, it was Cyrus who helped Angela hide her in the freezer. Before concealing the crime, he had been dispatched to their home when a neighbor complained of a strange odor stemming from the residence. The moment Cyrus knocked on the door, he knew immediately that the odor was rotten flesh. But one look at 17-year-old Angela's virgin body made him not care. He was in awe at her sexy round breasts, small waist and wide mouth. He immediately lusted after her, if he played his hand right she would be his sex slave, but first he had to help her dispose of the body. But how?

The answer came at a most mysterious way. His cousin, who sold stolen slabs of beef to restaurants on the side, was replacing his old deep freezer with a newer one. When the cousin brought the option to Cyrus he had an idea. For one hundred dollars, the old freezer was his. He took the freezer to Angela's house and together Cyrus and Angela placed Shannon's body inside, and went about life like nothing ever happened. As her body hardened from being frozen, the smell disappeared with time.

Six nights out of seven, Cyrus would leave his wife, and sneak to Angela's house on the other side of town. He would take her body freely, whether she wanted him to or not. She did every sick thing he desired, because it was the only way that she could keep her sisters together in their home.

When she turned 18-years old, Angela signed her mother's name on welfare checks and her sister's school documents, which eluded authorities. Although it made for a dreadful life, the plan worked, until the night Cyrus decided to cum inside of her body, instead of pulling out like she begged him to. Three weeks later Angela was plagued with a severe bout of nausea. Pissing on a pregnancy stick at school, she learned her fate, that she was pregnant.

Since he never gave her a lot of money, worried she would leave him for a man her age, she could not afford an abortion. She knew how he felt about children, because he threatened to beat the baby out of her if she ever got pregnant, so in her mind she was stuck. And now, because of his carelessness, Angela was dead, and her sisters were alone.

After murdering Angela, when Cyrus heard his fellow police officers footsteps upstairs within the house, he approached the deep freezer to be sure that Shannon's corpse was still inside. Quickly he opened the freezer and his jaw dropped. In the freezer were three little girls, with icicles forming on their upper lips.

He was just about to shoot them, and blame it on Angela to cover his tracks, when the officers rushed down the stairs, before he could pull the trigger.

With no time to waste Cyrus bent down and stared directly into Jazzy's eyes. "You the oldest so I'm holding you accountable for this shit," he whispered. "If you ever say anything about what happened here tonight, any of you, I'm gonna find you and your sisters and cut the buds off of your chests. And then I'll slice your throats clean. Am I clear?"

Jazzy swallowed and in a throaty voice said, "Yes, sir. You're clear."

CHAPTER 1
Jazzy
(6 Years Later)

POW. POW. POW.

The gunfire outside of my bedroom window startles me, but my boyfriend Cani (pronounced Can-I) keeps his hold of my waist, as we stand in front of the full-length mirror on my bedroom door. I'm naked, and the belt on his blue jeans rubs against my lower back.

"Your face" – he says rubbing his rough hand along my cheek – "is perfect. Your breasts" – he continues rubbing his hand along the bottom of my titties, and squeezing lightly – "are perfect." He pushes my long black hair off my shoulders, and the curls tickle my back.

"Cani, please don't—"

"Not until you look at your body the way I do," he whispers into my ear. "You're perfect to me, Jazzy. When I look at you walk across a room I'm thinking all the time that she's mine. *All mine.*" He looks at my belly and rubs his hands across my navel. "Your stomach, is perfect." He moves his hand over the sides of my hips, along the waves of my stretch marks, which I got from gaining and losing weight in the past. "Your hips, are perfect."

I look at the tiny black mole on my upper lip, and try to see in myself what he does. He makes me feel warm all over, and sometimes I feel underserving. "I love you, Cani," I say looking at his eyes through the mirror. "More than I ever knew was possible."

"I know, mami," he says as his hand holds my throat softly, like he's about to choke me, before he kisses the side of my neck passionately. "I know."

To look at Cani is to fall in love all over again. The light from the window bounces against his smooth chocolate baldhead, and silky black goatee. I believe if the human race died, and started all over with Cani being the father of all the children, the world would be beautiful. He's just that kind of man. But, sometimes I think he tires of my attitude towards myself. I think he wants me to be stronger, and I'm really trying, but it gets hard at times.

Earlier today I was having thoughts out loud, about him not loving me anymore, and finding a girl with a better body than me. Don't get me wrong, I have a thin waist now, with a fat ass and smooth legs to match, but it's not because I work out. Stress will do the same thing to you, if you let it. And, unfortunately I do.

Cani says he is in love with my body, but I'm in love with his too. He's much older than me at 30 years old, but we get along perfectly. He's the father figure wrapped up in the man I never had, and I'm gone over him. Head over hills.

Things are good. Real good, if only he would help me out financially around the house. I feel like I'm the breadwinner when it shouldn't have to be that way. As I look at his bare chest in the mirror, as he stands behind me, I think about the current state of my affairs.

FINANCES
BANK ACCOUNT: $54.32
ON HAND: $33.00

Tonight is Friday, which is payday. But every time it comes to him and my sister kicking out around here, I'm left to handle our bills by myself. They got lots of excuses to give me, but no money in hand. To make matters worst, we are already late on the rent, which is $500.00 a month, and management is threatening to throw us out sometime this week. If it wasn't for a little smooth talk we would've been homeless, but I convinced my landlord to give me a few more days.

My 19-year-old sister, Love, works with Cani at Cluck Buck Chicken on Allentown Road in Forestville Maryland. Love makes minimum wage, about $7.25 an hour, but still she's always broke. It's not because of household expenses. The only thing I make her give me is $50.00 a paycheck, since she brings home about $210.00 after taxes, but lately she doesn't even have that. Love doesn't have any bills so what gives? She'll do crazy shit like hand me $5.00 with promises to give me more money later in the week, and I'm always left wondering where her paycheck goes. She's not buying new clothes, or hanging out with friends, and to be honest I think she's a loner. Something is definitely going on, but I don't know what. It's quiet for awhile, until I hear my sister Love banging around in her room. She's always in there doing something.

I turn around to look into Cani's eyes. I run my hand over his warm baldhead. My heart beats faster because I hate having money conversations with him. "Baby, you know I told the rental office that I would give them the money on Monday. I think he's getting tired of me asking for cash. You kicking in tonight right? When you get paid?"

He steps away from me, sits on the dirty yellow windowsill and stares outside. "You know I'll do what I can, Jazzy, but lately things have been rough for me. I'm not holding out on you or nothing, but with my personal bills, and my mother hitting me for two hundred last week, I'm kinda broke."

I walk over to the bed, grab my white robe and cover my naked body. I step up to him and say, "Can I ask you something?" I look into his eyes, hoping he isn't growing frustrated with me. "I'm not trying to press you out its just...well...kinda important." I twirl a thick strand of my hair around my finger.

He wraps his arm around my waist and pulls me toward him. I sit on his knee, and we both stare out into the snow-covered neighborhood. "You can ask me anything you want, baby. You know that."

"Why is it...I mean...how come—"

"Sometimes they be shorting my checks, Jazzy. You know how them fucking Greeks be who own them Cluck Buck spots. They don't think niggas good for nothing but frying and flipping chicken. What you want me to do, rob 'em? Because I'll break the law if that's what you want."

"You know I don't."

"Then what is it?"

I don't speak.

"Try not to worry so hard." He kisses me on the neck again. I love when he does that. "I'm gonna do what I can, but I can't make them give me nothing they don't want too either. If I press them out about my checks, they might fire me before I get another job. I'm sorry, baby. I been thinking about leaving anyway, and applying for a job down FloorMart. With my experience I should be able to go in as a manager at the very least. I'm just waiting for a position to come available that's all."

I love Cani, more than anything in the world I do, but I hate this broke shit. Still, he holds me tight every night when the nightmares come down on me about how that mothafucka killed my sister. I need him with me, to keep me comforted. To keep me feeling safe, because not a day goes by where I don't think about Cyrus, and wonder if he's coming for me and my sisters.

When the police took us out of that freezer, on the day my sister was killed, the bottom of my feet were frost bitten, and Nandi's right toe had to be amputated due to being freezer burnt. After that, we had to stand in front of the court, and tell them that our sister alone placed our mother into the freezer for the welfare checks. I threw up for three days straight after lying on her, because I felt I dirtied her name. They put us in a group home, luckily together, where we slept in the same bed, despite having beds of our own. But the group home was worst, and back then I wondered if I should kill us all myself to stop the misery.

A year later, when I went to high school, I got a job at Smalls, a large grocery store in the Washington DC area. I had been there ever since, and now I'm an assistant manager, bringing in about $12.00 an hour on the days I *can* work. I call out more than I care to admit, and my supervisor clocks me in sometimes, because she understands my situation. It's not like I want to call off as much as I do. It's just that Nandi is sick a lot, and Tabitha, the girl who is supposed to sit with her when I go to work, calls off a lot. If she is not here to watch Nandi, I can't work, and so the broke cycle begins. Money is so scarce around here these days that I wonder how we even survive.

"Why you look so sad, baby," Cani asks me rubbing my thigh.

"I don't know," I shrug looking out of the window. "I guess I got a lot on my mind." I don't want to sound like a pest. I don't want him to know that sometimes I think he takes advantage of me, because he knows I'm afraid to be alone. "I'll be alright though. Don't worry about me."

"You wanna fool around before I go to work," he asks. "We ain't had sex in two days, and it's long overdue."

That's not what I had in mind, but I don't have a choice. He's my man and I must satisfy his needs. "You gonna wash it first right," I ask.

He pushes me away from him softly, stands up and walks toward the dingy yellow wall. He leans against it and looks into my eyes. A piece of chipped paint floats to the floor, and lands next to his bare foot. "Why don't you want to fuck me, Jazzy? I'm a man, and you a woman, so why don't it feel right when I'm trying to be with you?"

"I don't know what you mean."

"Yes you do," he yells. "How come every time we're about to fuck, you telling me to go wash my dick, like I'm some nigga off the street or something?"

My heart thumps in my chest. The look on his face scares me, and makes me think he's five minutes from breaking up with me. "I just...I just need you to wash it first that's all. It ain't like I don't want to make you happy in the bedroom, Cani. I do, it's just the way I like to do things that's all. It will only take you a second."

He walks up to me, grabs my shoulders and pulls me toward him. "What the fuck happened to you as a kid? Can you at least tell me that? Talk to me, baby. Instead of hiding what's on your mind and heart. What you can't trust me or something?"

"Of course—"

"Well talk to me then!"

A tear falls down my face. I want to tell him so badly. But how can I voice the answer in a way that won't make me look sadistic or crazy? How can I tell him that most nights after Cyrus finished having sex with my sister, he would come into my room and make me suck his dick clean? He would ask me, *can you taste your own sister? Her pussy is sweet right?* It does something to my mind just thinking about it. How can I tell him that I could still taste the inside of my sister, on my lips after he would cum into my mouth? I just can't, so I avoid the topic altogether.

"Cani, I'll have sex with you, and I love to do it too, but you just gotta wash it first that's all."

He backs away from me and frowns. "You know what, I'm done with this stupid ass shit. You being juvenile, and you act like you don't know how to handle a man. At first I thought you were on your shit, but I guess I was wrong."

He walks over to the wooden chair in the corner of my room. His white work shirt is folded up on the seat, along with his socks and t-shirt, just where I left them. Everything in my room is neat. For real, everything in my house is immaculate, despite the structure being a fucking mess. Cleaning my house is the only time I can focus and think straight.

"Cani, maybe we can take a shower together," I say walking up behind him. "I can wash you, and you can wash me," I smile rubbing the muscles in his back. "You love when we make love—"

BOOM! BOOM! BOOM!

The banging on the wall from my sister Nandi's room next door sends more yellow paint chips falling from the ceiling, and onto the wooden floor. "Jazzy," my sister yells from her room, "I...I can't breathe! Help me!"

CHAPTER 2
Nandi

I can't breathe. I can't breathe. I can't breathe! I'm
sitting in the corner of my room, on the cold wooden
floor, with my legs spread out in front of me. My air
feels trapped inside my chest, and I can't feel my finger-
tips anymore. They're numb, and I think I'm going to
die for sure today, until I see Cani's face as he walks
into my room.

He sits down in front of me, in the wooden chair, his
barefoot brushing against mine. "Baby girl, breathe,"
Cani says to me real softly. His face is getting blurry,
because I'm losing oxygen. "Jazzy, go plug in the
breathing machine." When Jazzy doesn't move, because
she's looking at me he yells, "Do it now!"

Jazzy quickly makes her way over to my machine. I
place my hand over my chest because it's hard to speak.
I want to tell her that it's broken, but no words are coming out of my mouth.

"It's not working," she says, flipping the switch repeatedly. "It's not coming on, Cani! What we gonna do
now?" She looks scared and that makes me more nervous. I want her to grab a hold of the situation. Sometimes my sister is weak, and I hate her for it. Does that
make me wrong?

"Love, go make some coffee in the microwave," Cani yells into the apartment. "Do it now. Nandi is having an asthma attack!"

I hear her running out of her bedroom. "Okay, I'm making it now," Love replies. "Give me a second!"

I can't breathe. I'm feeling lightheaded. I...I...

Cani places his warm hands on the sides of my face and smiles at me. Then he pushes my long black braids out of my face. He opens his mouth and sings, ♪*"I had some problems, and no one could seem to solve them."*♪ He's singing my favorite song in the whole wide world, *All This Love*, by El Debarge.

♪*"But you found the answer,"*♪ he continues, ♪*"you told me to take the chance and learn the way of love, my baby."*♪

I can't breathe! I can't breathe! I place my hand over my chest and my eyes close a little. The worst thing in the world is not being able to breathe. I wonder if this is how my fish felt when I threw him out of the water that one time.

I flop around on the floor, trying to save my own life, but it's not working. Why isn't it working? Suddenly I feel drowsy.

"Nandi, don't close your eyes! Just calm down, baby," he grabs my face more firmly, "I want you to try and relax for me. But whatever you do, do not close your eyes."

At that second my sister Love comes into my room, gives him the coffee and he snatches it out of her hand. Her bronze curly hair is wet, like she just hopped out of the shower. Hot coffee drops splash against my leg and he wipes them off. Coffee helps open my lungs, at least that's what the doctor said. With all that it does, I can never stand the taste.

"You're gonna be okay, baby girl," Cani says holding the cup. "I just want you to drink this, okay?"

He places a hand behind my head, raises the pink coffee cup to my lips and pours a little down my throat. At first I try to drink it too quickly and choke. I cough a few times.

"Slowly, Nandi" – he pushes my braids away from my face – "drink it slowly."

I do as he says, but I still can't breathe! I can't breathe! I'm scared. I'm thinking about dying. I'm thinking about how my sister Angela was killed. I'm thinking about Officer Cyrus, and if he'll come back soon and try to kill me, or my big sisters.

I'm going to die! I'm going to die!

"Nandi, you gonna be okay," Cani smiles, "trust me. Now please calm down."

"Here, use this," Jazzy says handing him my inhaler. "There's a little bit inside."

Cani presses it against my lips and I pull. She's right, there isn't much inside, but I take what I can. Within seconds I feel air filling up inside my chest. I feel stronger. I feel better.

I smile at Cani. To me, he's the most beautiful man I've ever seen in my life. He's so nice to me, and he treats me like I'm here, like I matter. When I don't feel well, he'll come into my room, and read me one of my favorite stories. Cinderella. Sometimes he and my sister Jazzy will read them to me together, and on those nights

I always sleep good. I love when they read to me. But more than anything I love Cani's voice. He can sing like an angel.

I swallow some more of the bitter coffee, and hand him back the cup. "Better," he asks me.

I nod, and smile wider. "Much better. But can you sing me the last part of the song that I like?"

"Of course, beautiful," he responds. Cani clears his voice and sings, ♪*"As the sun has its place up in the sky, I love you, so dearly. And all the same, there's no need to wonder why, I need you, please hear me."*♪

"Thank you, Cani," I hug him tightly. "Thank you so much."

Jazzy bends down and looks at me. I can feel the love in her eyes whenever she focuses on me. Like she wants to take all of my problems away, but doesn't know how.

"You can't do that to us again," Jazzy says pressing her cold hands against my face. "You almost gave me a heart attack. What happened anyway?" she asks rubbing her arms due to it being chilly in here.

"My breathing machine," I say pointing to the wall, "it's broken again."

"I know, but why did you need it, Nandi? Most times you don't have an attack unless you're worried about something. Is there something on your mind?"

"No, I'm fine."

She walks over to the dirty wall where my machine is plugged up. I hate it in here, but I know we can't afford to go no place else. When Jazzy thinks I'm not listening at night, and she's by herself, I hear her begging

God for some help around here. I hear her begging God to get us out of these conditions, and to give her a clue on what to do next.

If my lungs were strong enough, I would help her with the bills, and get a job, but I can't make it to my closet most times without losing air. I know I'm a burden. Even if I could get a job, I haven't been out of our apartment for years, and I cry when I have to go to the doctors. The world out there scares me.

"You think the electrical socket has a shortage in it again," Cani asks walking over to Jazzy. "You know Killion's the worst landlord to ever own property in D.C. The socket probably needs to be fixed."

Jazzy's shoulders rise and fall lower than they were before, as she eyes the machine. She seems heavy, like the weight of the world is on her shoulders. I hate when my sister feels like this.

"I don't know," she says under her breath. And then she looks at my partially open window, and her eyes widen. "Nandi, why do you keep opening this window," she asks angrily. "When you know the dust and dirt outside can sneak in here and catch you off guard? Triggering your asthma? That's probably why you had an attack." She slams the window shut.

"I wanted to hear the band play outside because I was bored, plus Loop was outside."

Jazzy frowns. "Dirty Loop didn't say nothing to you did he?" She approaches me. "I don't want you talking to that dope fiend. You hear what I'm saying?"

"He didn't say nothing to me, Jazzy, he just waved when he was coming into the building," I say. "And I said hi."

Loop was my sister Love's boyfriend. They told me when he first started coming around that he was supposed to be a big time basketball player. I don't know what happened though. One day he was walking around the projects wearing nice shoes, and bouncing a basketball, and the next he was barefoot and wearing dirty clothes. He fell real hard and never seemed to get back up.

"Well I don't want you talking to him, or waving at him, you hear what I'm saying," Jazzy says pointing her long finger in my face. "And don't open this window no more, Nandi. Promise me!"

"I promise," I say under my breath. My nostrils flare and I can feel myself heating up. Like I want to hit something or somebody.

She goes over to my dresser and picks up a pill bottle. "Why are your medicines getting lower and lower?" She shakes the Zoloft bottle and the purple Advair container.

"Your sister not trying to be mean," Cani says softly touching my arm, "but open windows are bad for your lungs. Your lungs are special, and we don't want you hurting yourself like that again. That scared me. That scared us."

"I got it from here," Jazzy says. "You gotta go to your job, Cani."

He focuses on the doorway in my room and yells, "Love, it's time to go to work! If you riding with me come on now!"

Love strolls into my doorway, rolls her eyes at him and says, "I gotta get my clothes from the laundry room downstairs first. Give me a few minutes."

He frowns and folds his arms over his bare chest. "How come you always washing clothes" – he frowns – "When its time for us to go to work? What are you really doing in that basement?"

"Nigga, the day I find out you my daddy will be the day I start answering your questions around here. Until then do me a favor and suck my clit," she yells.

"Love," Jazzy snaps, "don't talk to him like that, and don't talk around Nandi like that either. She don't need to be hearing your dirty ass mouth."

"Sorry, Nandi. The nigga be setting me off sometimes."

I roll my eyes at her. "Well I don't like it either. I don't like when you talk to Cani like that."

Love shakes her head and eyes Jazzy and Cani. "It's a shame how brainwashed ya'll got that girl when it comes to this nigga," she pouts. "Like I said," she continues looking at Cani, "I'm going to the Laundry Room, and I'll be back. Leave me if you want to, and see what will happen. You and I have an understanding. Don't we?"

CHAPTER 3
Love

I creep down the stairs, with the yellow laundry hamper in my hand, filled with shirts and a gray quilt. Once I make it to the basement, I turn left and walk toward the Laundry Room in the back of the building. When I'm there, I stand in the doorway before entering. I can smell the musty scent of the damp floor and moldy walls. It's scary in here, but I gotta go inside anyway.

I take a deep breath and walk toward the washer and dryer. The only light in here, stands above the machine, but everything around it is as dark as outer space. I place the hamper on the dryer.

"Loop," I say softly, looking into the shadows. "You here, baby?"

He steps out of the darkness and stands in front of me. He's wearing a dirty brown shirt, and holey blue jeans, but in my eyes he is still perfect. His hair is thick and fleecy, and it looks like he hasn't combed it in days. He probably hasn't.

"Hey, baby," he says stepping in front of me. "I love you."

"I love you too," I whisper. My knees buckle. He still makes me weak.

"I've been waiting on you to come, at first I thought you were about to let me down. I'm glad it isn't true."

My heart breaks for more than one reason. Before Loop got on dope, he was a star athlete in college. I swear I never seen anybody handle a ball the way he did, and people were calling him the next Michael Jordan. As a shooting guard he would leap, dunk and send a basketball flying into the hoop like nobody was on the court but him. He was God when he played ball, and he still is God in my eyes.

Everybody who knew us said we were made for each other, like stamps to an envelope they'd say. The only person who seemed to think he was bad news for me was Jazzy, and she didn't have a good reason why. She said he bragged too much, and men like him were never good for anything. But with the nigga who slept in her bed every night, she was the worst judge of character.

Anyway before long the Chicago Bulls announced their intent to pick Loop up if he entered the draft, and he was on cloud nine. We were so excited when we got the news, and I couldn't help but tell everybody I knew that my boyfriend was a future NBA star. By that time I had already dropped out of high school in the ninth grade, and didn't have a plan for my own future. Watching Loop play ball, was the highlight of my life, it was what I wanted to do for a living. Until Valentines Day, two years ago. It was the day everything changed.

That day rain poured with a heavy force, and Loop and I had an argument. I found out that Big Titty Tina, who went to Howard University with him, was hanging around his practice trying to get his attention. I guess she caught wind that he was going to be a draft pick, and wanted to put her bid in before he made it big. But Loop's cousin told me about the bitch's game, and said I needed to get him in line, because he was smiling in her face, like shit was sweet.

I went to approach him but he wasn't home. I went to his practice and he wasn't there either. I was afraid he would dump me, get with her and leave for the NBA, and I would never see him again. My stomach hurt all day, and I stayed on the toilet, shitting my life away. While I was at work, I called him again and finally he answered the phone. I cursed him out, and told him it was over even though I didn't mean it in my heart. I wanted him to fight for me, and prove he wanted me. But he didn't call me none after the argument, and I just knew it was over. So I left work early, opened the door to my building, only to see red rose pedals leading up the steps to our apartment.

For awhile I was shocked. My feet were planted in the doorway of my building, with rain dripping from my hair and purse. When Loop came out of my apartment, and stood at the top of the stairs holding a diamond engagement ring, I immediately started crying. This was the day I was waiting on but could never imagine.

"What is that," I asked pointing up at it.

"You know what it is."

"Loop, don't play with me. If you're playing I'll never forgive you for this shit."

He laughed. "Baby, I love you more than I ever loved a girl before. And I know I'm young, and people will try and tell me not to marry you, but I don't give a fuck what they think. I love you, baby, and if you'll do

me the honor of being my wife, you'll make my life com-
plete. Will you marry me, Love Law?"

"Are you serious, baby," I said crying harder.

"Dead serious," he laughed. "Now will you marry
me or not? Stop fucking around."

"Yes, but are you going to come down here and car-
ry me over the threshold?" It was stupid now that I
think of it, but I wanted him to do it so badly. It was
more about control than anything.

"I don't know, baby, it's a lot of steps and I don't
want to drop you."

"Please," I begged him, jumping up and down. "It's
Valentines Day, make the night right."

He was hesitant at first, but he eventually met me at
the bottom, lifted me in his arms and stepped on the first
stair. Loop was strong, and since I'm not a big girl, he
was able to carry me up the stairs with ease. But once
we made it to the top, he slipped on the rainwater and
rose petals, and lost his balance. I had never been more
scared in all of my life.

I tumbled out of his arms, but was able to grasp the
iron banister before I fell all the way down. Loop wasn't
so lucky. He slipped and tripped on the petals. He
seemed to hit each step, before eventually banging his
forehead and landing in front of the door. Blood poured
from the open gash on his head, and he was screaming
in pain. It was a nightmare, and I will always remember
his face.

I ran into the house, called 911 and prayed they'd
get there sooner than later. Nandi looked scared when
she saw my face, and kept asking me if she could do

anything to help. I pushed her away because nothing was more important than saving his life.

Before long help came and Loop was rushed to the hospital where we found out he broke bones in his back, legs, arms and hips. He was placed in a full body cast for a month, and couldn't move anything but his eyes. It wasn't long before a doctor told us what we already knew. That the injuries he sustained ruined his chances to play professional basketball. Loop was traumatized.

Before long we were able to see who his true friends were, when his dreams were smashed, and the hospital visits stopped. The physical and emotional pain he experienced on a daily basis was unbearable, so he was prescribed Vicodin. But as the days got darker, Vicodin didn't heal his pain anymore, because he needed something to numb his heart.

That's when I came into the hospital room one day, and saw one of Killion's dope boys at his bedside. A day after that Loop started using heroin, and that's when everybody really turned their backs on him. The price for Killion's first dope pack? My diamond engagement ring. He apologized everyday after I asked him where it was and he gave me the bad news. I didn't even care though, because it wasn't about that with me. I just wanted to be with him.

His family was different, they cared about the money. They knew that there was no possibility that he'd ever play for the NBA anymore. Without the NBA contract he was worthless to them. But, he wasn't worthless to me.

"I will never let you down again, Loop," I say to him in the Laundry Room. "I will always be in your corner, and I don't care what people say about you or our love."

He walks up to me and smiles. "You bring me anything, baby?"

I go through the hamper, move the quilt around, and pull out his bag of heroin. I hand it to him, and my arm trembles. His gritty fingers cover mine, as he takes the bag and he pulls me toward him. I can smell his dirty skin, and the funk of his infected gums rising from his mouth, still I don't care. He's my baby, and he's like this because of me.

"I love you," he tells me smiling at the package. "So much." He separates from me, spreads the quilt from the hamper on the cold concrete, next to the washing machine. He takes a seat, with his back resting against the appliance. He reaches out for me. "Come down here, and sit next to me, Love."

I should be getting ready for work, but times like this are special to me, and I want them to last. I would be lying if I didn't say that it turns me on that Loop needs me to survive. I'm his everything to him, and without my help he'd probably die. So I ease between his legs, and rest my back against his frail chest that use to be so muscular when he played ball.

"Do you remember when we first got together," he asks, rubbing my hair. "When you first told me you would be mine?"

I laugh. "Yeah, it was after you beat my boyfriend Brandon up, when you saw him walking to my house. I thought you were going to lose your career for what you did to his face."

He laughs. "He was a punk anyway, and you didn't need to be with nobody like that. I did you a favor by snatching you away from that nigga."

I giggle until I think of something serious. "If you never met me, you wouldn't be like this. Everything you're going through is my fault. Do you regret meeting me?"

He sighs. "I love the game, Love, I really do, but none of that shit would've mattered if you weren't in my life."

"Do you really mean it?" He doesn't answer. "Loop, do you really mean it?"

He's quiet now and I look back at him. His face is as blank as a white sheet of paper. He removes a needle from his pants pocket that he uses to shoot up. I sit up, turn around and look back at him. His eyes are as serious as a doctor performing open heart surgery, and I want to experience the feeling with him.

"Let me do it with you," I say. "I don't have nothing to live for without you, Loop. So let me try it. I want to do everything with you."

He frowns at me, and stands up. "Don't say that stupid shit to me. Why would I want you on something that controls your mind like this? I don't want this for you, Love, you know that. I don't want it for me either, but now it's too late."

"Please, Loop, let me do it with you."

"Love, get the fuck up out my face with that bamma shit," he says sternly looking down at me. "I'm not playing with you. If I ever find out you fucking with this shit too, I'm done with you. We through, forever. Do you hear what I'm saying?"

I stand up, and brush the back of my jeans. "How the fuck you gonna dump me when I'm the one who supplies your need?" I laugh to myself. "You can't do shit without me, Loop. If anything, you about to shoot up my shit. I bought that pack, not you. You should be kissing my fucking fect instead of standing over there popping shit."

He shakes his head. "Never underestimate the mind of a determined man." He pulls a spoon out of his pocket, along with a cotton ball and a lighter. I wonder what else he has inside there. "You don't know what I can do for myself, Love. You haven't been through nothing serious in life to know what it takes to be me."

My jaw flexes. "If you knew the turmoil I go through inside my mind on a daily basis, and how it felt to see my sister killed, while I sat on my mother's frozen body inside a deep freezer, you wouldn't talk to me like that."

I'm talking to him but Loop isn't mentally with me anymore. He is cooking his fix, and I stand back and watch in amazement. I look at his eyes, and the way he focuses on the poison in front of him. He's looking at it the way he use to look at my pussy, when I laid naked in front of him before we fucked. I'm jealous suddenly, and I wonder if I snatch it away, would he try to kill me. I think he would.

This is probably why my sister doesn't want me being bothered with him, and as far as she is concerned I don't have a connection with him anymore. So my relationship with Loop is private, and I prefer it that way.

When his cook is done, Loop raises the sleeve of his shirt and looks me in the eyes. "Can you tie me off, baby? Real tight the way I taught you?"

I ease toward him, happy to be involved. "Where is the tourniquet?"

"It's in my pocket."

I dig inside his jeans, remove the rubber rope and tie his arm securely. He taps his vein several times, and it pops up under his honey brown skin like worms under mud. He sticks the needle inside of his flesh and pushes the poison inside of his body. His eyes are on mine now, as if I'm sharing the moment with him.

Within seconds an orgasmic expression covers his face, and I wonder how he feels. He looks like he just came in his jeans. A long line of slob dangles from the corner of his mouth, and falls onto the quilt on the floor. His eyes close and his head drops backwards. My pussy tingles.

"Ahhhhhhhh," he moans. "Fuckkkkkkkkk."

I'm just about to ask him to use some of the dope on me, when I hear Cani's voice call out to me in the hallway.

"Love, its time to go to work! Where the fuck are you?"

CHAPTER 4
Jazzy

I'm sitting on my green living room sofa, staring at the front door. I'm dressed in my Small's Assistant Manager uniform, and waiting to go to work, but as usual Nandi's caregiver Tabitha, is not here. Irritated, I snatch the cell phone out of my red leather purse and text her.

Tab where R U? I'm running late 4 work. Call me back now or you're fired!

I throw my phone down and stare at the door again. Tabitha has a key and I'm praying to God that she uses it soon. If I have to call off of work again, it will be the second time this week, and I'm liable to lose my job.

Trying to keep my mind off of my drama, I jump up from the sofa, and grab the Ajax, washcloth and bucket from under the kitchen sink. Filling it with scalding hot water I drop to my knees and clean the floor tile by tile.

While wiping the floor I think about my youngest sister again. Although Nandi is 16, she has the mind of a child and I need someone to sit with her to be sure she is safe, takes her medicine, and doesn't get into trouble. It's expensive paying a sitter, buying medicine and paying the bills with a low paying job and no help. I guess that's why I'm stressed out all the time.

by Candee

When my knees are sore and my floor is clean enough to eat off of, I stand up and brush myself off. And then I pick up my cell phone again, and feel my skin heat up when I don't see Tab's response. This shit is driving me crazy!

When I first posted the position in the newspaper, for someone to care for Nandi, Tabitha was the last person I was interested in hiring. She came late for the interview, didn't have experience, and kept asking me about how much she would be paid. But when I met the other candidates, they were so awful that Tabitha was the lesser of the evils. Besides my job was pressuring me about my performance so I needed her ASAP, and she could start right away.

But it didn't take long for the bullshit to set in. Everyday Tabitha was calling off talking about her boyfriend was doing this, or her boyfriend was doing that. One time she called me crying. She said that her boyfriend said that if she didn't take him to work, since his car broke down at the strip club, that he was going to dump her and throw her out of his apartment. Although Tabitha's work performance was terrible, I was willing to deal with her, only if she was showing up, but soon she wasn't even doing that.

When my phone dings I quickly grab it. It's a text message, but I sigh when I see it's from my best friend Kaitlin, instead of Tabitha.

Girl, wait until U hear about my recent adventures. I'll C U soon. Luv U.

I don't respond to her, instead I hit up Cani. I don't like how he left this afternoon, with him thinking I don't want to have sex with him. It's just that sex is difficult for me. Being fucked by Cyrus messed my head up, and made me cold to men's sexual desires. It also bugs me out that with their dicks, they have the ability to ruin our lives.

If a man can fuck a woman, and get her pregnant, shouldn't he have to take care of the baby too? Some dudes don't feel that way. They think it's cool to sleep with a female, and stick her with the baby alone just because she's the one carrying the child. That's what happened to my mother and my father.

My mother met my father in Germany. They were stationed there in the army. Things were great in their marriage, and I never thought things would change for me, Angela, and Love. We had a big home, friends, and a settled life. But when my father met a younger, and much prettier version of my mother, he left us alone and moved her into his home. My mother was pregnant with Nandi at the time, and not even a month later we were out on the streets, a month before Easter.

My mother couldn't handle it when he filed for a divorce, and it wasn't before long that she turned to drugs. If my older sister Angela didn't step up after my mother's overdose, I hate to think what would have happened to my sisters and me back then.

Thinking about my father makes me think about my boyfriend again. So I text him to let him know he's on my mind.

by Candee

Me: Hey…
Cani: Hey

I look out in the living room, and try to think of what to type to him next. I can tell he's still mad, so I'm trying to choose my words carefully.

Me: I miss U babe
Cani: That's good 2 know
Me: Still mad?
Cani: Disappointed. Not mad. There's a difference.
Me: I'll do anything U want 2night. Just say the word

I wait for five more minutes, but he doesn't respond. I think he's done with me, and my chest tightens just thinking about our relationship being over, and sleeping alone in my bed at night. Then there's the thing I just said on the text, about doing anything he asks. If he holds me to it, I don't know if I can follow through or not. Cani is hungry in the bedroom and I always feel depressed when we're done.

When I look at the clock again I see I only have fifteen minutes to make it to work, and it takes me an hour on the bus to get there. I realize what I already know, she isn't coming. I have to call my job, and tell them I'm not going to be able to make it.

I pick up my cell phone, and notice I still don't have a response from Cani. He's over me I'm sure of it. *Sigh*. I don't need this stress today.

I call my job and my supervisor Lauren answers the phone immediately. "Uh…hi, Lauren, this is Jazzy."

"Hey, Jazzy, how is everything going?" Her voice sounds heavy, not warm and upbeat like it usually is.

"Not too good—"

"Jazzy, please don't tell me you aren't able to make it to work again, darling. The general manager is here and he's scaring me. Making me think I won't have a job if I keep letting people have the weekends off. Now you know that you have my support with Nandi, because I realize you're doing a lot on your own. But I'm asking you to help me out tonight, and show up for work," she pauses. "Please."

Before I heard the anxiety in her voice I was going to say I couldn't make it, but now I can't do that to her. "I'll definitely be able to make it," I say. "I'll just be late that's all."

"Oh, dear," she sighs, "Jazzy, please come in as soon as possible. I'm begging you."

"I'll be there, Lauren. I promise, try not to worry," I say hoping it's the truth.

The moment I hang up, Tabitha is walking into my house with an attitude. She's a chunky girl, who loves to wear clothes too small for her large frame. For instance she's sporting a tiny white leather coat that exposes her brown belly, and tight blue jeans that show the buckles in her thighs.

In a hurry, I grab my black leather coat, purse and meet her at the door. "Tabitha, oh my God, I can't believe you are running this late. My boss is expecting me there like yesterday."

"I'm sorry, girl, but my boyfriend was late dropping me off tonight. We had a fight outside your building and everything. I started to call off, but I knew you needed me to be here for Nandi. You know I try to help you out when I can."

Help out? Bitch this is your job. "Well I'm glad you're here but now I have to bounce," I say, "Nandi is in the room sleep. Try not to wake her up."

"Can I have my money before you leave," she asks. "Brian is downstairs and wanted to borrow a couple of bucks from my paycheck. He's taking it to the liquor store. I hate to do this to you now but I'm kinda strapped."

I frown and say, "Not until I come back." I turn the doorknob and open the door, before she can dispute. "I'll see you later." I slam it behind me.

That bitch must think I'm crazy. I wish I would give her-her paycheck so she can leave Nandi in there by herself. No bitch, I'm not that stupid.

The moment I step into the hallway, I run into Starr, my horny next-door neighbor. She is in heat so much dogs hang out in front of our building. She's wearing a little silver negligee, and slippers with feathers on them that match. Her brown titties are spilling out of that outfit, and it's obvious she ain't selling shit but pussy.

"Hello, Jazzy, where is that fine ass man of yours?" she looks behind me at my closed door.

"Didn't you get enough of asking about my man, after he slapped you in the face for disrespecting me? You need to get you some business, Starr, before somebody hurts your feelings for real. Or put you out of your misery."

She rubs her thighs and laughs. "He sure did hit me," she grins, "but it didn't bother me one bit, I love it rough. You should stop being so square and toss things up a little too. If you ask me, that fine ass nigga of yours looks bored."

"Bye, bitch," I say running down the stairs to catch the next bus.

"Bye, beautiful," she responds.

I hate her so much I can scream. One day somebody gonna take care of her, and I hope it will be soon.

The moment I open the door leading to the office at the grocery store, I can hear the General Manager's raging voice. He's going off on Lauren. I don't walk inside right away, because I get so embarrassed when he chews Lauren out in front of her employees. She's 60 years old, with curly gray hair, and it just seems wrong for a 6'4, 300 pound Italian man to be yelling at her like she's a child. He has no respect.

"So let me get this straight, you allowed five employees to call off, despite it being Friday, the busiest day of the week," he says to her. "Please help me understand, Lauren. Is that what you did?"

"Y-yes, sir," she stutters. "They couldn't come in. They all tried but different things were going on."

"And just what were the reasons they told you that they couldn't come in this time," he responds. "I've got to hear this shit."

"Uh…well…Jennifer's daughter is running a high fever…the high one hundreds I think. Spencer's car is broken down on the side of the highway, and he was waiting for roadside assistance. Daffany's aunt is in the hospital because her pacemaker isn't working…they don't think she's going to make it. And uh…uh…Courtney has the flu and Wendy's grandmother just died."

The general manager burst into laughter. "So you mean to tell me that Wendy's grandmother died and came back to life three times? Is that what you want me to believe?"

"I-I don't understand," she stutters.

"That bitch's grandmother has died five times already, you old hag," he yells. "Don't you see that they are taking advantage of you? Because you let them? Or are you naturally that stupid?"

The way he talks to her causes my stomach to churn.

"What about Jazzy Law," he asks her. "Where is she? Since she seems to be the only responsible one around here."

I'm no better than the others but for some reason he gives me passes and it makes me uncomfortable.

"She's coming, she's just running a little late that's all," she says.

The moment she says that I receive a text from Nandi.

I woke up by myself. Where is Tabitha?

Oh fuck!

CHAPTER 5
Nandi

I'm sitting in the corner of my bedroom, looking at my open door. Tabitha left me home by myself again, and I hate being alone. What if some strange man comes into my room, and shoots me like he did my sister Angela? I don't wanna die. I want to stay alive, read my books, and look out of the window to watch the time pass me by.

Now I'm having a hard time breathing! I'm having a hard TIME BREATHING! Whenever I get scared I can't breathe. I need some air! **I need some air!**

I crawl across the wooden floor, rise to my knees and open the window. A cool breeze blows inside and makes it frosty, like I'm standing outside. I take a deep breath, and the cool air rushes up my nose. I feel better already.

"Nandi," someone whispers from below, outside of the window, "hey, Nandi. You up there?"

I look down, to the ground, and Mr. Johnson who always sings to me is outside smiling up at me. "Hi, Mr. Johnson," I say waving.

"Where is Jazzy?" He always asks about her, and Love, and if they here or not. "She home from work yet?"

"No," I shake my head from left to right. "Jazzy still gone."

45

"What about Tabitha," he asks as he removes his dirty black hat, and scratches his graying woolly hair, "she up there with you?"

"No," I shake my head again, "she left too. A little while ago. I'm all alone."

He smiles now, and I can see all the dark places where his teeth are supposed to be in his mouth. "You want me to sing you another song," he asks, "maybe the one Cani sings for you all of the time? The one you love so much."

Cani has the best voice in the whole wide world, but Mr. Johnson got the second best. I always wondered how a man who looks the way he does, can sing so good. Maybe God gave him that voice, since his face not so pretty to look at.

I grin and say, "Yes, I'd like for you to sing the song please. It would make me very happy. Do it like you did it last time…and hit the high levels."

He places his hat over his heart, like he's about to give allegiance to the American flag. His mouth opens wide, and he's singing something, but I can't make out the words. Usually his voice is so loud, that I have to back away from the window, because my ear drums vibrate. But, no he's singing so soft, I can't hear nothing.

"Your voice too low," I say. "I can't hear you."

"Let me come upstairs, that way I can sing in front of you, and in person. It won't be no trouble, Nandi. No trouble at all. I have a cold and my voice is hoarse now that's all. But if I'm in front of you, it will be better."

My heart beats fast. Jazzy told me to never talk to strangers, and whenever I don't listen to her, something bad happens. "You can't come up here. I'm not supposed to have people in here my big sister don't know. I'm sorry, Mr. Johnson, but that ain't gonna be possible."

"Now you hurting my feelings, Nandi," he says pouting. "Haven't we been friends for a long time?" His arms drop by his sides. "Ain't you did stuff for me that only friends do for each other? And ain't I did stuff for you, that you'll want me to keep secret forever?"

"Yes," I nod, "I think so."

"Well how you gonna say we don't know each other? We friends, we best friends if you ask me."

I smile widely. "Really?"

"Of course we are," he says placing his hat back on his puffy hair. "Look, it's a little too cold out here. I really wanna come up there, and sing for you, so I can warm up for a little and you can hear my voice better. I'll just be in the hallway, Nandi. It ain't that serious, trust me. You don't even have to open the front door. I'll sing to you out in the hallway."

I want him to come up, I really do, because I get bored a lot. Sometimes I make up stuff to do, but when I'm done, I'm bored all over again. So it would be nice for him to sing to me, I just don't want him to come inside.

When I was a baby Angie use to sing to me all the time, I guess that's why I like it so much now. I would fall asleep about the second verse of every song. I miss my biggest sister. I miss her a lot. Too bad she got taken away from us by a bad cop.

I look back out of the window at Mr. Johnson and say, "You can sing in the hallway, but I can't let you in the house. I'm sorry, but I don't want my sister Jazzy to be mad at me. She told me never to let anybody in, plus I don't walk out in the living room anyway, so I wouldn't be able to open the door for you even if you did try to come in. I hope you understand."

"Don't worry about nothing, Nandi. In the hallway and nothing else, unless you want me to come inside. I'm coming up right now," he says opening the building door.

I close the window and sit back in the corner. The floor is colder now, because the window was open so long. From my bedroom I can see the front door clearly. I just hope he doesn't try to come inside, and I hope he keeps his promise.

But the moment I think we got an understanding, the gold doorknob jiggles rapidly back and forth. Mr. John-son lied to me, just like Mr. Cyrus. He's trying to get in here. He's trying to hurt me! Sweat pops up on my fore-head, rolls down my face and falls onto my upper lip. My heart is beating rapidly inside my chest, until I see Kaitlin, Jazzy's best friend, come through the front door.

Kaitlin has short black curly hair, and a face like a model. I never seen Kaitlin's hair or makeup out of place, and it looks like she may have somebody to do it for her professionally all the time. She's wearing a shiny black coat, and shiny black high heel shoes too. They look plastic, but she still looks cute in 'em.

"I don't know where the fuck you were headed, but it better not have been up in here," she yells at Mr. Johnson, as she holds the door open. "Jazzy don't like strange mothafuckas in her house when she not home, and she definitely don't fuck with your begging ass."

"Wasn't nobody 'bout to go into Jazzy's house," he says to her. "I was just about to sing for a friend that's all."

"Johnson, go somewhere and kill yourself," she says, "before I do it for you," she slams the door in his face. "Dirty ass mothafucka." She still looks upset as she throws her purse and coat on the floor, until she looks at me in my room. A huge smile extends across her face, and she approaches the door. Although she comes close, she doesn't enter. "Hey, Nandi, so that bitch left you in here by yourself again huh? That's a worthless human being if there ever was one."

"Uh huh," I respond. "She said her boyfriend was outside."

"What a piece of trash," she shakes her head, "I swear I keep telling Jazzy that good dick," she clears her throat, "I mean, good help is hard to find around DC. Maybe now she'll listen to me. So how you feeling, kiddo? Can I get you anything? Food? Drink? Anything at all?"

Kaitlin has a way of talking to me like I'm a baby, like I don't understand what she's saying if she speaks normally. I don't like regular people, but I understand them more than they know.

"I'm fine," I say rubbing my neck, "my chest was hurting earlier that's all. It's cool now."

"Well where is your breathing machine," she looks into my room from the doorway, "and inhaler?"

"My machine is broken, and I'm almost running out of the stuff in my inhaler."

"Damn," Kaitlin says under her breath, "I guess Jazzy still falling on hard times right? That's sad. If she act right, I may have a way she can earn some money, but that's gonna be on her."

I shrug. "I don't know about her money problems. She ain't said nothing to me about it."

"Well I remember what to do for your chest," she says dipping off toward the kitchen. "Give me one second! I got you, Nandi. Don't worry one bit, Kaitlin is here."

I stand up and walk to my doorway. I never leave my room, unless I'm going to the bathroom right next to it. And most times I do that when nobody is at home, or fast asleep. I feel safer that way. From here I can see her bustling around the kitchen, open and closing cabinets and drawers, like she's looking for something special. When it quiets down a little, she comes back with something in a cream coffee cup.

I back away from the doorway. "Can I come in," she asks me.

"No." I don't want her in my room. I don't want her in my space.

She seems a little down. "Well here you go," she reaches her arm into my room, but stays outside of it. "It's for your chest."

I walk up to her, take the cup out of her hand, and sit back in the corner. When I look inside, I notice it smells differently. Not as strong as coffee should be. "This tea?"

She goes to her purse and takes something out, "Yeah...why?"

I laugh. "I think you meant to give me coffee instead. This doesn't help me."

She burst into laughter and says, "Please forgive me, Nandi, but I'm far from the maternal type, although I try to be sometimes." She shrugs. "Let me go make some fresh coffee for you now. Where do you guys keep it?"

"That's okay," I say, sipping the bitter tea, "I'm already feeling better." I sit it on the floor next to me. It's too gross. She didn't even put sugar inside the cup.

Kaitlin lights a cigarette. My eyes widen, because I can't believe what she's doing. Cancer sticks to me, are like Kryptonite to Super Man. They just don't mix. I think right away I'm about to die.

I'm standing in my doorway again, watching my big sister and Kaitlin in the kitchen. Jazzy's eyes are so wide they look like they're about to pop out of her head. "Girl, what were you doing, trying to kill my sister or something," Jazzy says to her, after she smashes the cigarette out in the sink. "You know she can't be around all that smoke and shit. Sometimes I swear you think with your titties instead of your brain."

She runs the water for a minute. Then grabs disinfectant and starts cleaning the counters. Our apartment is really old, but it's also really clean, thanks to Jazzy's obsessive ways.

"I'm sorry, girl," Kaitlin says, "I got a lot on my mind. Something that was supposed to pan out a few weeks ago didn't go as planned." She walks into the living room and sits on the sofa. Jazzy sits next to her, and removes one of her tennis shoes. "And it's still fucking me up, because I thought I had the situation in the bag."

"What's up?"

There's one good thing about being invisible sometimes. People forget you are around, and often say things in front of you that they normally wouldn't if you were relevant. That's what's about to go on now, I can feel it. So instead of standing in the doorway, I slide down to the floor, with my back against the frame. I'm trying to be so quiet, I don't even blink.

"So you know I was working Mark Stanfield over right," Kaitlin says leaning back into the cushions of the sofa, crossing her legs.

"Yeah, you talking about the dude who was just drafted for the NBA," Jazzy responds taking off her last shoe.

"Yeah that good for nothing ass nigga," she sighs. "Anyway, I had the boy just where I wanted him, Jazz. I'm talking about he was eating my pussy while I pissed on the toilet, fucking me raw and everything else. Until he got wind that he was about to be put on with the NBA. Now all of a sudden things are different between us, and when we make love he want to be all extra careful and shit. Yelling about he gotta use condoms now."

"So," Jazzy says.

"So...how am I gonna get pregnant if he too overprotective when we fuck? I missed my big break, Jazz, don't you see what I'm saying?" She throws her hands up in the air. "And to make matters worse, since we had a fight about using condoms, now he's leery of me all together. He don't answer my calls or nothing when I try to reach him. I'm talking about the nigga cut me off smooth!"

"Damn," Jazzy says, "well, at least you can say you had him."

"Bitch, that ain't about nothing! I wanted to have his baby," she rubs her belly, "fuck the bragging rights. Do you know that one child by that nigga sets me up for life? Man, I want his baby so badly I'll be willing to pay somebody to help me." I see the strange look she gives my sister but she doesn't notice.

Jazzy laughs. "What you mean pay somebody to help you?"

"It's like this, Jazz, the nigga thinks I'm dumb but I'm not," Kaitlin says tapping my sister's knee, "he got a thing for young nerdy type girls, but will fuck the freaked out ones like me for points and to bust a nut. I know plenty of whores, what I don't got a lot of is good clean girls like yourself lying around. If I can just get somebody he fucking to slide one of them wet condoms off of his dick, and give it to me, I'll be in there like swimwear."

"Ugh," Jazzy frowns backing away from her, "I can't get down with all of that shit you talking about. You'd do better to get a job and focus on your own hustle, I mean really Kaitlin, have some self respect."

"Why I don't have self respect? Just because I want a little nut? I mean come on, Jazzy, it don't cost nothing to take it from him. He practically giving it away for free! It's there for the taking. You can do it for me, Jazz. I know you can."

She points to herself. "Me?" She giggles. "Are you really coming out and asking me to do this type shit for you? When you know how I am?"

Kaitlin shakes her head. "I forgot about you, and your Dick-Washing-Ways. So after all this time, you still don't want a dick nowhere near your pussy or mouth? Really, Jazz? After all this time? I mean what does Cani say about this good girl gone nun behavior? You might as well turn lesbian."

"Whatever! And Cani don't like it but it ain't nothing he can do about it neither," Jazzy shrugs. "It's just how I feel. It's just how I am."

"But why? What happened?"

"Girl, it's a long story, and over drinks one day maybe I'll tell you. Just know that for now it ain't going away. And even if it did, I wouldn't play myself like this. I'm sorry."

"I'm not gonna lie," Kaitlin sighs, "I *was* going to ask you if you could get the nut for me. I took an ovulation kit the other day and everything. I'm about to ovulate, Jazz. Probably in the next few days. All I need is the nigga's sperm, and I'm good. You can be a rich little auntie and all of my problems will disappear. Think about our future!"

"They got ovulation kits?"

"Fuck yeah," Kaitlin continues. "At every pharmacy you can think of. Anyway, it's saying that within the next few days your best friend is going to be fertile and ready to get pregnant. If you do it for me, and get me the sperm, I'll give you $500.00, Jazz. Cash money in hand! I know you can use it."

"Girl, I'm not with no crude shit like that. I just have to press Cani and Love to start helping me out around here with the bills, that's all." She pauses. "I planned on having a conversation with her and him anyway, since I had to call off of work. Who knows how many times my boss is gonna take my shit."

"That's what I'm saying! It's money in your hand now," Nandi continues. "Not later. You can use it!"

"What if he gives me HIV, or AIDS?"

"The nigga is clean, I saw his health records. And I got some non-spermicidal condoms at home, Jazzy. I'm talking about I got this entire gig laid out in my mind, I just need the star of my show, and that's where you come in. I know you can use the money too, and not just for the bills. Nandi told me her breathing machine broke and she needs another inhaler. This paper will help you out. You in a bind, friend and I got you!"

"Oh shit," Jazzy says standing up looking at me, "I forgot Nandi was in the doorway."

Dang! She remembered me.

"Nandi, go in your room, and close your door. I don't want you to be hearing all of this shit."

But I heard it already. I stand up and prepare myself to walk towards my room.

"She good, you ain't talking about nothing I want to hear anyway," Kaitlin says. "You might as well let her hang out."

"As long as you not talking that dumb shit. Don't ever bring no nasty stuff like that to me again," Jazzy says. "Racy things like that are not my style, and you know me better than that."

My sister's phone dinged and she grabbed it off the table. The look on her face turns to frustration.

"What is it," Kaitlin asks her. "Everything okay?"

"It's Love, she just texted me and said she lost her job."

"Damn," Kaitlin says.

CHAPTER 6
Love
(ONE HOUR EARLIER)

I'm in the break room at Cluck Buck Chicken, leaning against the wall, with my arms crossed against my chest. All eight of my co-workers are here too, dressed in white and yellow chicken suits, looking like a bunch of idiots. We all do. I hate this fucking job!

Cani's manager, Rod Paulson, is standing next to Cani at the head of the table. "I know this is coming at a bad time, with Christmas around the corner and all, but we have to let a lot of people go," Rod says.

"Let a lot of people go?" one of my co-workers repeats. "When is this supposed to go down?"

"It's effective immediately."

"This some bullshit," Mike Rooks says to him. Mike has been out of jail for only a month so he doesn't know how to talk to people yet. "I just got this fucking job, my probation officer gonna flip the fuck out when he hears this shit!"

Mr. Paulson looks like he turns a bright red, and I love it. "Sir, you can't use—"

"Don't tell me what the fuck I can do," Mike yells, yanking the chicken cap off of his head, and throwing it on the cherry wood table. The beak on the chicken's head squeaks. "I knew this job was some bullshit." He stands up and approaches Rod who is now trembling. "I know one thing, I better have my check by tomorrow, or I'm coming back to kick your ass," he says stabbing his index finger into Rod's chest, "and you too," he says pointing at Cani. Mike storms out of the room, and slams the door behind him. It takes everything in my power not to laugh.

Rod wipes his sweaty forehead and looks at Cani. "Well, I'm about to leave," Rod says clearing his throat. "You can handle it from here right?" he hands Cani a stack of papers. I guess he's leaving him to do the dirty work.

"I have it," Cani says to him. "Don't worry about anything."

Rod looks at all of us and says, "Cani over here will give you all of the information you will need regarding your employment status. Good luck, and merry Christmas."

What a fucking loser!

As Rod walks out of the room I grow anxious. I swear to God I hope my name is in that stack. I hate this job, and only kept it as long as I did to get money for Loop's dope. But, I have another remedy for that situation, which works better for me anyway. My plan will require me not to have to lift a finger.

When I walk closer to the table, where every one else sits, I see my name on one of the slips in Cani's hands. I smile, and wide too. One of my co-workers nudge me and asks me what I'm happy about. I ignore him. He's not about to bring down my high all because he wants this little bullshit ass job, to have enough money to get fat Carey who comes in here everyday to suck his dick. I'm on cloud nine, and he ain't gonna take that from me. But then something happens. Cani separates the slip with my name on it from the rest.

"Give me a second, everybody, I'll be right back."

He walks out of the room and I wait impatiently for the status. From the window on the door I see Cani talking to Rod again. Cani whispers something into Rod's ear. Rod looks at me, snatches the sheet out of Cani's hand and balls it up. I feel the air escape from my lungs. Once again Cani has proven to be a pussy. And despite how my sisters feel about him, I can't stand him. He's a no-good ass nigga who doesn't deserve my sister's love or attention. And the sooner Jazzy realizes it the better we all will be.

When he's done ruining my life, Cani walks back into the room, winks at me and calls the name of the people who lost their jobs. Most of them, have the same reaction I do, they seem to care less. When everyone who is fired leaves, I sit in the seat and look at Cani. Hoping he's saving my name for last, and that I will still be jobless so I can file unemployment.

"Your name was on the stack too," he says walking over to me, like he did me a favor. "But, I had Rod get rid of it, so you could keep your job." He sits down, and a chair is between us. To me that's not enough space, and I want him further away.

"I didn't ask you to do that," I tell him.

"To do what?"

"To get my job back."

He leans back in the seat, and crosses his legs in a manly way. "You didn't have to ask me, Love. We family."

I frown. "Cani, you are not my fucking family. There's nothing 'bout you that I like. You know that, because I've told you many times before to your face. So if you gonna get in the business of doing me favors, you better stop now. It's a complete waste of time."

He sits up straight and stares into my eyes. "Why do you hate me so much?"

"Uh let's see, because you fucked our next door neighbor in our house, and when Nandi walked out and caught you, you convinced her into believing that you smacked Starr in the face for disrespecting you, instead of on her ass cheeks, like we both know you did when you were hitting the pussy. Except, you didn't know I was home, in the closet, looking at everything under the door. You are so good at brainwashing Nandi, that she even convinced my sister of the story."

He grits his teeth and balls up his fist. "If you hate me so much why didn't you tell?"

"Because I wanted you in my pocket, and I know my sister ain't ready to let you go just yet. It's gonna happen soon though. I can't wait."

He lowers his head. "I made a mistake, Love."

"Tell me something I don't know."

"What do you want me to do," he screams, causing me to jump back into my seat. "Leave your sister? Because if I do that, it's going to break her heart. But I'm so tired of this shit I don't even care anymore. Is that what you want?"

"You know that's not what I want."

"Then what can I do," he screams louder. When someone walks past the door, and looks into the window, he lowers his voice. "Listen, I don't give a fuck about Starr. That bitch is trash to me, and I made a mistake. Men sometimes do. Pussy is our weakness."

"Tell me something I don't know." I shake my head. "The funny thing is, my sister set you up like a hero. I'm talking right next to Superman and Batman. But I know the truth. You no better than any other nigga, just more attractive," I say. "Then again, that's your weapon ain't it? Your looks, and that slick ass tongue of yours. You probably can convince anybody of anything you want, can't you?"

"If that was true, we wouldn't be sitting here," he sighs. "Love, what can we do to rectify this situation? What can I do to make things right? I'm confused."

"I'll tell you how it's going down. We gonna do two things, first you gonna tell my sister that I lost my job."

His eyebrows rise. "But, I got your job back."

"I don't want my fucking job back," I yell. "I can't stand being here, or around you. It's bad enough I have to see you at home. I can't take no more of your smug type face at work too."

"Love, your sister needs help with the bills around the house. And if you're taking my checks as blackmail—"

"Which brings me to my next point," I say, "The second thing you gonna do is give me half of your checks as usual. If you don't do both things, by backing up my lie about losing my job, and continuing to give me money, I'll tell Jazzy everything I know. I'll tell her how Starr makes you pay money out of your check each week to take care of your illegitimate son, Aaron, who Jazzy doesn't know about. And most of all, I'll give her the play-by-play, on how you fucked Starr in our house, over the edge of our couch." I grin. "I'll tell her everything, I promise."

He sighs, frowns and then moans. "What were you doing in that closet anyway? You could not have seen everything you did, if you had not been in that closet."

"Don't worry about it," I tell him.

"I'm going to find out what you are hiding too, and when I do you not gonna be the only person with shit over a nigga's head. Believe that."

CHAPTER 7
Jazzy

Cani is in the kitchen rinsing the cooked noodles off in the sink, before pouring them back into the silver pot on the stove.

"Did she take it real hard, when she lost her job," I ask him. I'm sitting at the kitchen table looking at him prepare dinner. He's making spaghetti and meat sauce, one of our favorite meals, mainly because it's so cheap.

"Yeah," he says dryly.

"What did she say exactly," I ask. "Because when she called here earlier she sounded like she was going to cry."

He places my plate in front of me, and his plate on the other side of the table. Then he grabs a white paper plate out of the cabinet for Nandi. "Jazzy, Love is a grown woman, and I know why you feel like you gotta protect her, but that just ain't the case no more. You need to start allowing her to be accountable for her own decisions, and her own life."

What he's saying causes me to boil with anger. He doesn't know about the things me and my sisters have been through. Love is just as emotionally fucked up as me and Nandi are. I'm not about to make shit worst by giving up on her.

"Cani, I'm just asking what she said to you that's all. I want to know how she handled the news. You don't know my sister the way I do. She's angry all of the time for no reason, and she lashes out. If she carries that with her out on the streets she might get into trouble."

"Tell me about it," he says making Nandi's plate.

"What the fuck is that supposed to mean?"

"Give me a second," he walks into Nandi's room, hands her the plate.

"Thank you, Cani," Nandi says to him softly.

"You're welcome, sweetheart," he replies before closing her door and walking back into the kitchen. He looks at me and sighs. "I think you need to let Love get a place of her own. It's time for her to move out, if we gonna work out."

My lips tighten. "So you want me to give up another person I care about."

"I know you're not about to bring up that situation again."

I sigh, bringing up the past probably is a bad idea. "Cani, it's not a good time."

"Why not? I know she was talking about moving out at one time, when Dirty Loop was clean, and off drugs. She still wanted to leave but you stopped her, and put her on a guilt trip. Maybe you should humor the idea again."

I stand up. "Humor that idea? What the fuck are you talking about?" I go into the kitchen to wipe away two sauce spots that dropped on the stove. My apartment is old, but it's definitely spotless, and I like to keep it that way. I grab the Pine Sol from up under the sink and slam it on the counter. "You're so use to walking away from family that you don't know how to stand up and fight no more." I run the hot water and grab the kitchen rag. "Love needs me, and I'm not going to abandon her." I dip the rag into the scolding hot water, pour the cleaner on the spots and wipe them off roughly.

"Jazzy," he says walking behind me and wrapping his arms around my waist, "Love is trouble. Do you hear what I'm saying, she isn't good for you. And I want a family of our own, and I'm afraid that if Love stays around, she's going to pull us apart. Look at how much we fight around here."

I throw the rag into the sink, turn around and look into his eyes. "Don't try to make me choose between you and my sisters, Cani. If you love me you would never do that. When my sister was murdered I promised to never abandon them, and I kept that promise all the way up until now. Please."

"You're right, baby," he says kissing me on the neck. Then he gives me those bedroom eyes that scare me and make me smile. "I know I made dinner, but how about me and you go makeup. We been fighting all day and I'm tired of it. And when we've worked up an appetite, we can eat."

"Okay," I swallow, "maybe we can jump in the shower first and play around a little bit."

He backs away from me, slips into his sneakers and grabs his coat. He has an attitude, and his face twists up in anger.

"Where you going, baby," I say as he moves for the door.

"To find Love, since she's the only one you care about around here."

CHAPTER 8
Love

"I'm glad I left that job, baby," I say to Loop, as I sit between his legs, while we lean against the washing machine in the dark Laundry Room. "People coming in there for bullshit ass food, yelling in my face when they don't get free shit, and stuff like that. I can't take it no more. Before they were laying off I was thinking about quitting anyway."

"You shouldn't have quit, Love," he says. He just had another hit, after I bought him some dope from Brandon, my ex-boyfriend and one of Killion's dealers. "You should've kept your job. I hate when you move without thinking."

"Why you say that?"

"Don't you want to leave your sister's house, and have a place of your own eventually? Or do you want to stay with her forever?"

"You know I want to move."

"Well you can't do that without a job. You know that."

"You don't get it, baby, because you don't have to work there." I turn around to look at him. "It's degrading when your friends come up to your job, and see you wearing a Cluck Buck hat with a chicken sitting on top, like you some strange ass cartoon character or shit. I never wanted to work there and only stayed to help out Jazzy. I'm done with that life though."

Loop kisses me on the ear, and his chapped lips scratch against my lobes. "Baby, you gotta grow up. It's time."

I sigh. "Maybe I'm not ready to grow up, Loop. I ain't like I had a chance to be a kid. Remember? It was taken from me when my mother started fucking with drugs, and my father left us. I feel cheated."

"Every time I hear you going through shit, it reminds me of my life."

"What you mean?"

"If I was better, and not on this shit, you would be set up for life," he says. "You wouldn't have to worry about anything. I'm talking about you would be rich. Man, you remember how I use to dunk on them niggas on the court? Wasn't nobody fucking with my game, baby. Shit by this time if I would've got signed, we would've been in Miami somewhere, in a condo overlooking the water." He squeezes me tighter. "Then my baby girl wouldn't have to worry about standing behind no cash register, and taking chicken orders. She'd be on the beach, looking sexy, laying in the sun and enjoying life. *Our life*."

"Are you mad at me, Loop, about Valentines Day? Because I asked you to carry me up the steps?"

He doesn't respond.

"Loop, are you mad at me?"

"Get up, Love," he says to me roughly. He disconnected from me again, and I hate when he does that.

"I'm about to take another hit. I got some shit on my mind I'm trying to push back."

I crawl away from him, stand up and move out of his way. I think about my boring life while he sets up his kitchen. I hate being in that apartment all day, hearing Jazzy fuck Cani through thin walls, or my sister talk to strangers out of her bedroom window. I want an adventure. I want to push the limits, even if I gotta take drugs to get me there. I want Loop to be the one to show me, but if he doesn't I'll do it myself.

I step closer to him and say, "I want to try it, Loop. I want to go where you are when you leave me mentally. Let me do it. Let me do it with you."

He takes the spoon out of his pocket, and throws it onto the top of the washing machine. It makes a loud clinking noise. "I told you to get up out of my face with that dumb shit, Love. This over here ain't for you. So get your eyes up off of it."

"If you don't let me do it I'll do it myself," I tell him. "I'm serious, Loop."

"Baby, please stop fucking with me about this shit tonight," he says throwing the rubber rope on the machine, "I got a lot on my mind right now. You don't know what a nigga thinks about on a regular basis, when he got nothing but time on his hands.

"You don't know how it feels to be sleeping outside, because your family don't fuck with you no more, and your woman gotta take care of you, while you hide in the basement and pray she doesn't abandon you. Leave me alone with this shit right now, Love, before you see another side of me you ain't seen before."

"If you don't let me do it, I'm gonna get a pack from Brandon up the block. You know he been trying to fuck me ever since he found out you were on hard times."

"So you back with Brandon, the nigga I took you from," he frowns. "The nigga who runs with the boy Killion?"

"I'm not back with him, but I will be if I have too," I say.

He throws the dope pack on the machine and looks over at me. "You foul, Love. Real foul."

My heart breaks. "But I don't want to deal with him, Loop," I step closer. "I wanna be with you, and be apart of your world. You love this shit," I tell him looking at the brown gold in the plastic baggie. "So I want to see what it's all about. I want to do it with you. And if you don't let me, I'll get it from someone else."

He sighs, wipes his hand over his forehead and looks over at me. "Love, please—"

"I'm serious. Either do it with me, or I'll do it alone, either way I'm getting high."

"Fuck," he yells, staring up at the pitch-black ceiling. "You got a clean needle?"

I smile. I got him. "I think I still got one of the new ones I bought for you," I walk to the hamper on the dryer, and move the clothes around to find it. "Here it is."

He rips it out of my hand, looks over at me again and says, "Come here, baby." I walk to him slowly. "I can't believe you making me do this. I'm gonna have nightmares about this day, Love, because this shit is life altering." He shakes his head. "Roll up your sleeve." I do. "You sure you want to do this shit?"

by Candee

"I want to be wherever you are, and if this shit means a lot to you, I want it to mean everything to me too."

He preps the drug and I wait anxiously. When he's done, he brings the syringe over to me, filled with brown liquid. "Give me your arm." He places the syringe between his teeth, ties the rubber thingy around my arm and pulls tightly. It pinches my skin a little and I whence. I don't have enough time to say I change my mind, before he taps my vein and sticks the needle into the flesh of my arm.

I see my blood go into the syringe and am a little freaked out at first. But, it doesn't take me long to see what all the hype is about. The first sensation I experience is bliss, like nothing bad has ever happened to me. Like I didn't walk into my sister's blood, after I stepped out of the deep freezer, the day she was murdered in the basement.

My entire body tingles, and when I rub my arms, goose bumps run everywhere. I bite my bottom lip, and moan. It feels like a full body orgasm. Yesssssss. Yesssss. This is what I wanted to feel all my life. Heaven. I'm in heaven!

"You okay, baby," Loop says touching my elbow.

When I look at him he's no longer Dirty Loop who lives in the basement, not that he ever was to me. He's transformed into the Loop I first met who was destined for greatness. Who was destined for the NBA, and suddenly I'm turned on. I want to fuck him, right here and now.

70

"Baby, are you okay," he asks me again. "Talk to me."

I want to speak but I know my words will be gibberish. Anyway I can't describe the sensations going through my body. Simple words won't do. Instead I lean against the washing machine, slide down to the floor, and freeze in place. I'm in ecstasy; I'm in another world. And if I know nothing else, I know I will do this shit again.

"Welcome to my world, baby," he says looking down at me.

I grin and say, "Thank you for letting me in. I feel like I'm finally home."

CHAPTER 9
Cani

Cani sat on Starr's brown leather sofa, looking up at her cute face, and outrageously curvy body, as she stood in the kitchen fixing drinks. The moment he stepped into her apartment, he understood how he got caught up with her to begin with. Starr was a sexy young thing, with a wet mouth and wetter pussy. Still, she was trouble, and he was definitely done with her as far as sex was concerned. At least he hoped.

"Starr, I love Jazzy, and I'm sorry I led you to believe it would be anything more between us, on the day we fucked. And I know because of it, I gotta help you take care of our son, by giving you what little cash I can. But, I can't keep giving you most of the money out of my paycheck each week. Jazzy needs help around the house with the bills, and its time for me to start kicking in. Please tell me you understand that."

Starr stepped out of the kitchen, wearing a pair of red and brown leopard print tights, and a black lace bra. The red lipstick, which covered her mouth, was already shiny, but she ran her tongue over her lips anyway, to make them sparkle.

"You know I'm not trying to make things harder for you, Cani," she stood in front of him and he caught a whiff of her sweet pussy. "I like Jazzy, and only want to make things comfortable for you," she handed him his

drink and he sat it on the floor. She did the same with her drink. "You know that my only aim is to make you smile."

"Then prove it," he said, trying to ignore her sex appeal. It was mission impossible though, considering his dick was rising like fresh dough inside an oven, within the fabric of his jeans.

"I'm gonna let you off the hook," she said, "you don't have to give me no more money for Aaron, except on the first of the month." She dropped to her knees and wiggled between his thighs. "He live with my mother anyway, so it ain't like she don't have a husband and some help around her house. He's good."

"Are you serious," he asked over excitedly. "You not even gonna hit me up today?"

"Nope," she said shaking her head slowly from left to right. "All the money you got in your pocket, you can keep. Consider that my gift to you."

He didn't have much, since he gave $130.00 to Love, but at least he could hold onto the $92.00 he had left. Maybe he would buy some pizzas and stuff tomorrow for dinner.

"You don't know how much you looking out for me by doing this shit," Cani said. "I really appreciate this deal, baby girl."

"I'm glad, daddy," she said lowering the zipper on his pants, "but you gotta do something for me too. Some gifts in the world aren't free you know?"

He swallowed when he felt the cold air rushing against his dick, since it was exposed, and out of his pants. "What is it? What you want?"

by Candee

"Well you know how much I like to fuck," she said kissing the tip of his dick, "and how much I need it everyday. You been with me that one time and you saw how I curved to you."

"Yes," he said wishing his dick would go down. "I know what you like."

"Well if you promise to come over here once a week, on the days you were supposed to give me my money, to give me some dick instead, I'll keep our little secret safe. I'm talking about taking it to my grave."

"Starr, I can't—"

Before he could finish his statement his dick was between her warm lips. He would be lying if he said that in the back of his mind, he wasn't thinking about fucking when he first got there. He just hoped she wouldn't jump out there so fast.

Besides, Starr was the exact opposite of Jazzy. She didn't care about how dirty a dick was or where it had been. She liked to fuck, and she liked to fuck hard and all of the time. When they first had sex, Cani had his dick in her pussy and ass, yet she still licked it clean.

"Raise up, baby," she said to him. "I want these jeans down by your ankles, so I can get this thing nice and wet."

Cani quickly fulfilled her request, before she could change her mind. It wasn't like he was going to be in any deeper shit with Jazzy, by getting some head. Jazzy would be just as mad about him fucking her the second time, as she would if he fucked her once. It was best to relax and go with the flow.

When his bare ass was on her leather sofa, Starr gripped his stick into her hands again. Then she pursed her lips, and blew a soft blast of air onto the tip. He stiffened up even harder, with the sexy motion. Starr's slimy tongue slithered down his balls, before she sucked on his nutsack like a cherry.

"You taste as sweet now as you did the last time," she complimented him.

Cani closed his eyes and let her do her thing. He could feel the softness of her cottony hair, brush against his thighs. Starr licked him for as long as he could take, without busting a nut inside her mouth.

"I'm ready for my present," she said standing before him, with a dripping wet pussy.

Starr lowered down on him, and his dick parted her strawberry-pink pussy lips as he pushed into her tunnel. When the feeling got better, Cani gripped her waist and fucked her like she was his bitch, and the pussy had his name on it.

"Beat this drum, Cani," she yelled a little louder than he wanted. "Fuck it good too."

"Don't say my name, beautiful," he suggested. They were in the living room, not too far from the door, and he didn't want somebody walking in the hallway and hearing his name. "Let's keep what we do in here between us."

"I'm sorry, honey," she said wiggling her hips. "I'll mind my tongue, but this dick is just too good to be true."

Cani lifted her up, and bent her over the arm of the sofa. The juice from her wet pussy fell from his dick and slapped against the hardwood floor. Spreading her legs wide, like he was the police, he rammed his thickness deeper into her body. When he felt the tingling sensation take over, he pawed at her breasts, and used them as reigns to go harder.

He was in heaven until he heard someone screaming outside of the apartment. "Help me, somebody help me! My sister just overdosed!"

It was Jazzy's frantic voice, and his heart dropped.

CHAPTER 10
Jazzy

"Cani, I don't want to hear this shit right now," I say to him, while we're sitting on the bench in the waiting area of the hospital. The noise of shoes scratching against the cream linoleum floor is driving me crazy. "You telling me that Love fucking with heroin is not right, and it won't help the matter. I know it's wrong, what the fuck I want to know is why she did it?"

"Why you yelling at me, baby?"

I roll my eyes. Don't get me wrong, I love him, but Cani is starting to work my last nerve. I need his strength not his bitchiness and I'm tempted to tell him to kick rocks. "I'm yelling at you, because you coming at me hard and crazy now. My sister could've died tonight. The least you can do is give me a little support."

He sighs loudly, and the lady next to us looks over in our direction and shakes her head. *Nosey ass bitch.*

"I'm sorry, Jazzy," he says rubbing my back. "I'm just mad that you going through this shit right now, that's all. I'm your man, and I worry about you." He looks out ahead of him, at all of the people coming and leaving the room I guess. "If it's not one thing it's another. One day you gonna be able to look out for yourself, and not have to worry about everybody else."

For some reason when he said that, I secretly hoped for the day, and felt bad about it seconds after.

"I didn't even know she was still dealing with Dirty Loop again," he continues.

I run my hand down my face. I'm frustrated, and disappointed in Love. Why would she want a nigga on heroin? It's like she's doing this shit to spite me. Ever since Angela died, Love treated me more like the enemy than her big sister. My hands are tied with her and I don't know what to do anymore. This day is hell! I mean, one minute I was kicking it with Kaitlin, and the next minute, Loop was banging on my door telling me she O.D'd.

'She passed the limit, Jazzy, she passed the limit,' Loop kept saying. *'I don't know, but I think she wanted to kill herself, and I don't know why. Can you tell me why?'*

No I couldn't tell him why! Maybe it had something to do with whatever happened in that hallway, when he fell down the stairs, causing him to lose his career. Nobody ever gave the details to me, and I didn't care to ask.

Anyway, Loop was a mess, and tears poured out of his eyes like raindrops from the sky when he said Love OD'd. That was the first time I could see he cared, because before that moment I thought it was all a joke.

There was more than one reason why I didn't like Loop. It wasn't just because he was arrogant, and bragged to everyone with ears that he had made it to the NBA, and would be leaving the hood behind. But, I also didn't like him because I knew who he really was, despite never telling Love.

One day Loop was outside, bouncing his basketball in front of our building, waiting on Love to come home from work. The windows were open in the house, because the air conditioner was broken, and I could hear Loop talking about how niggas could kiss his ass once he became a millionaire. The sound of his ball bouncing and his mouth rapping, rang throughout every room in my apartment, and no matter how loud I blasted Rhianna's CD, I couldn't escape the noise.

After about fifteen minutes, when I looked out of the window to tell him to shut up, I saw he was entering the building with some chick up the street. I put on my sneakers, and left the apartment to find out what was up. The situation looked weird to me. From the top of the stairs, I didn't see them next to the mailboxes, which meant I had to investigate further.

So I walked downstairs, and into the Laundry Room. When I got there, although it was dark as usual, I could clearly see him fucking Big-Titty-Tina from the back, while grabbing her long brown hair roughly. That alone was enough to make me sick to my stomach, but when I saw Tina's balls banging against the washing machine, I lost my bagel and eggs from the morning. Big Titty was a man, and Loop was bisexual. I covered my mouth, and crept back up the stairs without him ever knowing that I saw who he was about.

An hour later, when Love came home, I saw Loop kiss and hug her outside of the window. I was so sick to my stomach, I could barely move. I wanted to tell her what I saw, but I honestly didn't think she could take it. Loop was her everything.

by Candee

Later that night, when she came in the house by herself, I told her to leave him alone, because he wasn't
good for her. She quickly let me know as loudly as possible that that would never happen. Then she slammed
the door, and was gone for two days.

I heard Nandi weeping in the room, after Love and
me argued, and Cani had to sing to her just to calm her
down. It was an awful night but a few days later, Loop
fell down the steps in my building, and almost lost his
life.

I never told Love, even though I wanted to, about
what Loop had done. Besides, I thought she wasn't
messing with him anymore after he got on heroin, at
least that's what she told me anyway. Now I was starting to think that I made a big mistake, by never telling
her what kind of person he really was. If I had, she
probably wouldn't be here.

"I didn't know Love was dealing with Loop either,"
I tell Cani. My eyes land on the nurse, who admitted her
earlier today. I wonder does she have any more information for me. "I mean, how could she look at him everyday, when he fucks with drugs? I don't understand."

"I guess you can't help who you love," Cani says.

"That's not true. You can control who you love if
you really try, and you believe in your heart that the person is not meant for you. But, you have to be serious
and never see the person again."

"Jazzy, people don't fall in and out of love at the
drop of a dime," he says. "If you love someone, I mean
truly love someone, you will always be in love with

them. No matter what they do right or wrong in their life."

I hear him but I'm too angry to give his words too much thought. Until I remember something. "Where were you, Cani? Where did you go when you left the house, because it's obvious you didn't go find Love?"

"What are you talking about," he asks moving uneasily in his chair. And now that I look at him, I mean really look at him, I notice something is off, but I can't place my finger on what it is. "I went exactly where I told you I did."

"You left after making dinner, and said you were going to find her, but you didn't. So I'm asking where did you go?"

"I did try to find her. It's not my fault I didn't check the Laundry room, Jazzy. I mean how the fuck was I supposed to know that she would've been in there? It doesn't make any sense."

"Ms. Law, can you come with me," the nurse interrupts, "the doctor wants to see you about Love."

I get up and follow the nurse to another room, and Cani is on my tail. She takes us to a small office, where a light blue examination bed is dressed with white paper. I take a seat in the only chair inside the room. Everything seems so bright and cold, and I'm uneasy. It doesn't feel human, or filled with any kind of compassion, and I brace myself for bad news. I gotta move. So I stand up and walk next to the Anatomy of the Human Body chart and wait.

"I wish this mothafucka hurry up," Cani says pacing.

I wish he would just sit down, because if the doctor comes in, the door'll hit his ass.

"They shouldn't do people like this," he continues. "I mean if the doctor isn't ready to talk, why call us in here?"

I don't know where the tears come from, but all of a sudden I break out into a hard cry. It feels like ocean waves were rolling through my stomach, and rising up into my head. I'm crying because I'm broke. I'm crying because I feel weak. I'm crying because I don't know what to do, or what is wrong with Love. And, I'm crying because I know I don't have all of the answers, and probably never will.

"Oh, baby, don't worry about it, Love will be okay," Cani says, gripping me into his arms. I smell a strange scent on his shirt, and I'm disgusted. "I'm so sorry about this shit. You shouldn't have to deal with this alone, don't worry though, we gonna work it out—"

"Ms. Law, I'm Dr. Eaton," he says opening the door. When he sees me crying he stops in midsentence. "Am I interrupting something?" He looks at me and then Cani.

"No, no, I'm fine," I say wiping my face. "How is my sister?"

"She's recuperating. And as you know she had a heroin overdose. Right now she's still experiencing muscle spasms, and a slightly weak pulse. We do believe these complications will clear up, but we'll have to keep her overnight just to be sure. I hope you understand."

I swallow, and brush my hair away from my face with my fingers. "How much will it cost?"

"I'm not sure, but I don't think you need to worry about that right now. The important thing is that she gets the proper care, and help she needs."

Wow. So it's gonna cost me that much...

"Okay, is she up now?"

"Sure, she's up, but I called you here for another important matter. Is it okay to talk in front of your friend," he continues looking at Cani.

"What...uh...yes...of course," I reply nervously. "What's wrong?"

"You may need to watch your sister closely, she's showing signs of depression. And I was tempted to have her committed, but wanted to talk to you first. I asked her if everything was okay in her life, because often patients use heroin as a method to kill themselves. She said things are fine but she didn't seem forthcoming."

I think about Cyrus.

"Maybe you can take her on a small vacation, and get away from the neighborhood," the doctor continues. "When she returns, possibly seeing a psychiatrist might help too. The main thing you need to do is keep her calm, and away from drugs. We have detox programs, that can help her but she doesn't want the bed at the center. Maybe you can talk some sense into her."

I think about what Loop said, about her wanting to die, and my body trembles. "I'll try. Where is my sister now?"

"She's in her room, I'll take you there."

As I follow him out of the office, and down the hallway, things seem to move in slow motion. For some reason I don't want to see her right now, because I don't know if I can take it. I don't have any answers.

When my phone buzzes inside my pocket, I take it out and see it's my home phone number. I left Kaitlin with Nandi, after I found out about Love, so I hope everything is all right. Nandi can get into trouble if you let her.

"Hello, is everything okay," I say.

"Yes, Jazzy," Nandi says, "I was calling to tell you that there are policemen outside, I see them from the window. Lots of them. Something happened to somebody in our building. Can you come home? I'm scared."

I just got off the bus, after being told I have to come in now by the GM of Smalls Groceries. I know I need this job, believe me I do, but my mind is not on work right now. With Nandi needing a new breathing machine, and the doctor saying that Love needs a vacation, I need to be grateful for the opportunity that just fell into my lap. But, I don't know if this is really for me anymore, because I need to see what's going on at home.

When I make it to the parking lot, I see police cars everywhere. What the fuck is up?

When I walk inside, I decide to stop past one of the cashier's registers, to see if she could put me on to why the GM was trying to promote me, when Lauren already had the job.

"What's going on," I ask her, as she bags the groceries for her current customer. "Why are they promoting me?"

Ebony swings her long gold braids out of her face, and looks back at me. "Oh...hey! Congratulations, Jazzy," she sings. "I knew you would be up next, it was just a matter of time."

"I haven't accepted anything yet," I tell her, grabbing the paper bag out of her hand, to bag her customer's purchases, since I'm standing over here anyway. Besides, I needed to do something with my hands.

"That ain't what I heard," she says running a frozen pack of spinach over the scanner. "Folks is telling me that you on deck and that you already took the job. Sounds to me that if you want this job, you gonna be the boss, the Assistant Manager days for you are over."

"Can you tell me what the fuck happened," I ask holding a cold half-gallon of butter pecan ice cream in my hand. "I mean where is Lauren? If they giving me the job, I know she's taking it pretty badly."

"Oh shit, you really don't know what happened 'round here," she says taking the customer's credit card. "You must live under a rock. Lauren jumped off of the building, in the back of the store earlier tonight, they saying suicide, but I think that customer...Crazy Aaron, might've pushed her off or something. You know he been stalking her. That's why the store is flooded with cops right now."

"Lauren is dead?" I ask with my jaw hanging low. I can't put another thing in the bag, and Ebony takes over from there. I'm shivering too badly.

I'm stuck. Lauren was the best manager I ever had, since I'd been working here, and I don't understand why she's gone. She was a sweet old lady who took care of her three grandsons alone, because their mothers had taken a trip to Mexico and never returned. This is so sad.

As I'm standing in awe at her register, upon hearing the news, the general manager, who verbally abused Lauren for years, walked up to me. He thinks I never notice his sexual glances, but the way he eyes my body is always evident over the greasy stare on his face. The GM is a tall white man, in his late forties with a thing for black girls with big butts. I guess that's why he's fucking with me.

"I guess you heard already," he says to me as I try and busy my hands again and throw the last item in the bag, a can of creamed corn.

"I heard just now," I say as dryly as possible.

"Well when can you start," he continues, looking at Ebony's butt now.

He's so fucking gross! I hate him!

"I'm not sure. I gotta see about some things at home first."

He clears his throat and walks closer, stealing my comfort zone. Taking away any coziness I would normally have of this being my body, and that being his. I feel violated.

"Well we're going to need you to think quickly, Jazzy," he says. I can smell the garlic from the eggs he probably ate earlier on his breath. "The good thing about the old hag jumping to her death is that I don't have to look at her wrinkled face anymore. Now you," he says rubbing my lower back, out of view of Ebony, "you got a face I can stare at all night long."

Upscale KITTENS

I felt the first shiver on my left toe, but before long my entire right foot was shaking, and then my entire lower body was trembling with anger. Lauren was a nice person, whose only crime was taking his shit and looking out for her crew. That wasn't the only thing Lauren did to help out her employees, and this you might not believe but it's true.

When Anita Greene, her employee, needed a kidney, because she was the sole provider of her 10-month old daughter, it was Lauren who gave her one, putting herself out of work for one week. She wasn't just a good person, she was a saint, who probably killed herself because of how he treated her. She loved this job, and she loved the people too, and it was just wrong for him to speak about her like that.

"Get the fuck up out my face you bitch ass nigga," I tell him, after giving the customer her paper bag.

He steps back, and gives me the room I wanted before he violated me in the first place. He lowers his head, frowns and asks, "What did you just say to me, Ms. Law?"

"I don't want your fucking job," I tell him. I look at Ebony and wonder how her jaw hangs as low as it does without touching the dirty floor. She seems shocked; maybe she'll like the job better than I do. "This life ain't about shit, and I'm gonna find something greater."

I walk toward the door. "If you leave out of this store, Ms. Law, there's no coming back."

I think about the breathing machine. I think about Nandi and her medicines. And, I think about the apartment. Staying here, and taking the promotion would answer all of my financial prayers. But, I can't take the abuse from him so to me it just ain't worth it.

"Don't worry, I won't ever come back here, I don't care what I have to do to get money."

When I make it to the bus stop, I sit on the bench and cry. I feel immediately like I've made a mistake but the damage is already done. My head is throbbing, and the girl talking on her cell phone next to me, about how she fucked her cousin's boyfriend last night, is annoying too.

I shake my head, grab my cell out of my pocket, and send an important text.

Kaitlin, I'm gonna accept your offer for the $500.00. Is it still available? 'Cause I need the money.

CHAPTER 11
Jazzy

I'm sitting on the sofa, looking out ahead of me. Yesterday was a weird day and I still don't understand what is happening to my family. One minute I was employed, and my sister Love was clean, now I'm unemployed and my sister is addicted to heroin. To make matters worse, she's in the room with Loop, like she didn't just overdose, and like she pays the bills around here. She's supposed to be at the hospital, so why is she home?

I want to go in there and tell him to get the fuck out. Because, I need to talk to Love, so I can find out what's going on in her mind, but the doctor said she's been feeling suicidal, and having the type of conversation I need, may set her back again. I feel like I'm walking on pins and needles!

That's not the only thing going on. When I made it back last night, I found out that my next-door neighbor, Starr, was murdered in her apartment, and I don't know who did it. The police came over, and asked if I knew of any enemies who may want her dead, but I couldn't help them, because I disliked her too. I was smiling a lot at the detectives just to keep my name off of the list. I don't know a person alive who threatened her more than me.

by Candee

Apparently her big toe held her door open, and when Mike Joe who sells bootleg CD's came into our building to push his product, he saw her red toenail polish, and let himself into her house. He said she was naked and stabbed to death, with her tongue hanging out the side of her mouth when he left. He called the police right away to let them know, but they gave him six hours of interrogation for his trouble, before eventually releasing him the next day. He's still a suspect even though we still don't know what happened.

"Are you okay," I hear someone say behind me.

When I turn around I'm looking at my baby sister Nandi. My eyes feel like they are expanding because she never leaves her room for anything or anybody. As a matter of fact, I usually have to pull her kicking and screaming out of the apartment, when she goes to the doctor's. So seeing her like this was different, and it scared me.

"Nandi, what are you doing out of your room?"

"Checking on you," she says rubbing my hair, softly from front to back. "And making sure you're okay. Can I do anything to help?"

"Nandi, I'm fine." I stand up and approach her. "You shouldn't be out here. Go to your room."

"I'm going back," she says looking at me strangely. "I just want to make sure you're fine that's all. I wanted to make sure that all of your troubles are over."

My eyes widen and my heart rate increases. "What do you mean?"

"Are you and Cani still fighting," she asks, "because I tried to make things better. Did I?"

Loop comes out of the room as we're talking, so I'm not able to figure out what she means. My anger goes up another level, when I see his bare chest, and Cani's work pants dressing his lower body. Loop has sores visible on every part of his body. Round, burgundy sores that looked rubbed down to the muscle like they are trying to heal but can't. He scratches his dry chest, and his fingernails leave white trail marks over his nipple. I hate this man! And I want him out of my house.

"Ya'll got some water," he asks me after yawning.

"What the fuck are you doing here," I ask stepping up to him. "I don't want you in my house, Loop. You know that. I've never liked you before and what you did to my sister is wrong. Why would you let her do what's obviously killing you?"

"Jazzy, it wasn't even like that. You gotta believe me."

"All I know is that before you she didn't fuck around with dope, and now she does."

His hands drop by his sides and he looks down at the floor. I follow his stare, and my eyes land on his feet. They are coal black, a complete opposite of the honey brown spots on the rest of his skin. He's a mess all over.

"Jazzy, I love—"

"Don't tell me you love her," I scream, waving my hand. "I don't want to hear your lies. If you loved her you would not have allowed her to be put through this shit. Do yourself a favor, do all of us a favor, and get the hell out of my house."

"I can't do that." His voice is low but I heard him all the same.

"What do you mean you can't do that?" I frown. "This is my fucking home and I want you gone."

"Jazzy, if I leave, and am not here when Love wakes up, she's gonna be hurt. You know that. The last thing we want is for her to be stressed out. It's not good for her."

"I don't care," I lie.

"Well let me put it like this," he pauses, "Love's name is on this apartment too, remember? You put it there when you were trying to get pre-approved, because you couldn't afford it on your own name and income. That makes me Love's guest, and that means I can stay."

"You motha—"

"I don't want to fight with you," he interrupts. "I just need you to know that I'm staying here with my girl, and there ain't nothing you can do about it. And, I'm gonna get clean, and I'm gonna help her get clean too. We good for each other, Jazzy. You'll see! And if you can't…well…there ain't nothing I can do about that neither. I love her, and I'm sorry you can't be happy for us." He points to the fridge. "Now can I grab some water?" I don't answer, but he takes it as his queue and slides into the kitchen anyway.

It's not until I turn around that I realize Nandi is still there, and looking at him in the kitchen. I place my hand on her shoulder, and push her softly, so she can walk toward her room but she doesn't move. "Nandi, lets go." Her eyes are fixed on him. "Nandi, come on now."

Finally she looks at me and gives me that smile I love. Once in her room I go to her medicine tray, because it's time to take her meds. I grab one of the pill bottles and notice it seems light. "Nandi, where are your pills? The Percocet?"

She sits on the floor, in the corner of the room and says, "Gone."

"Why?"

She shrugs. "I don't know."

If somebody is stealing her meds, I already know that Loop had something to do with it, and I had plans for him later. He can fuck Love all day long, but he better not be messing with Nandi's shit.

"I can take care of him you know?" Nandi says to me. "It won't be a problem. I can take care of him just like I took care of Starr, and the others. It's fun actually, and gives me something to do."

My heart makes a strong rhythmic sound. I think I'm going to have a heart attack and I sit on the edge of Nandi's bed, which she never uses, because she prefers the floor.

"Nandi, what do you mean take care of him? And what do you mean like you took care of Starr?"

"I don't like people messing with my family. You know that."

I close the door and walk back over to her. "Nandi, what did you do?"

She doesn't answer. Instead she picks up her Cinderella book and proceeds to flipping the pages. "You know what I did, big sis. Don't play dumb now. You of all people know how I can be."

CHAPTER 12
Love

When I open my eyes, I feel something warm behind me. It's not until I turn over that I see Loop's face. He's sleep. I'm surprised that his skin smells of soap, and he doesn't look lazy in the face, like he doesn't have control over his facial muscles. He looks clean, and I wonder if he did this for me.

"Loop," I say softly.

He opens his eyes. "Hey, baby. I love you."

I eye him, and softly touch his face. When he smiles at me again, I kiss him on his lips, and when our lips separate, I can tell he brushed his teeth too. I feel like I'm home in his eyes. Like everything is okay now. Like this is real and everything else was a nightmare.

"Hey, baby," I say. "I love you too."

He pulls me toward him and my forehead brushes against his chin, before finding its way against his chest. I can hear his heartbeat, and it's not as fast as it normally is. He's alive. He's alive and he's in my bed, and I thank God.

"How long have I been out," I ask him.

"On and off for five days." He kisses my forehead. "How do you feel?"

"Weak. And my mouth is dry too. Can I have some water?"

He reaches over to grab a water bottle on the table. I
see a bunch of empty bottles next to it, and I figure I've
been drinking all day. "Here you go, baby," he says,
"Drink as much as you can."

He places the spout against my lips, and pours the
water into my mouth. I swallow so much that the water
drips from the sides of my lips and falls over my breasts.
I wipe it away, and finish the rest, but I'm still thirsty.
When I'm done he sits the bottle down with the rest of
the empties.

"You can't do that to me again, Love. You don't
know how it felt to see you spazz out on the laundry
room floor like that. You had foamy shit all over your
mouth, and I couldn't see your eyes anymore. They
were rolled up into the top of your head, and the only
thing I could see was the white parts. You know what I
would've done if you would've died? I can't take this
world without you. Had you not been by my side I
would be gone already."

"You would've been fine," I say, hoping he'd carry
on with how much he loves me. It makes me feel good.

"I'm serious. I would've killed myself, Love," he
says. "I'm nothing without you. You're my everything,
baby, you know that."

"I wasn't going to die," I laugh. "It was just a bad
reaction. Next time we gotta be more careful that's all. I
probably had too much for my first time. I mean you
took some too, and you didn't OD."

"I didn't take any of that pack, Love. As a matter of
fact, I haven't had any dope since you OD'd. I'm
through with drugs. This shit opened my eyes."

"So you saying Brandon gave me some bad stuff," I frown.

"I'm saying it doesn't even matter because that was a wake up call, and we done," he gets up and walks toward the wall. He leans against it and looks down at me on the bed. "I'm clean, baby. Like I said, I haven't fucked around, and I haven't felt this good since before I started that shit. I don't want to ever go back to the dark side again. I feel powerful, and aware now. That experience brought me back alive."

His eyes light up as he tells me his story of how strong he is, and how he feels he can conquer the world. But all I'm thinking about is the feeling I had in that laundry room. The feeling I want repeated. Anything that can transport you to a different world, when everything else around you is bad, is good enough for me, and I couldn't wait to do it again.

"Baby, don't get all crazy on me. We had a little bad shit, and that's all."

"Bad shit? You almost died, it was worst than just bad! And then your sister been on me every day since you been out, talking about she wants me to leave. Love, we gotta leave this apartment: We gotta get a new place of our own, baby. And, I been looking for jobs and everything."

I laugh so hard at him my stomach muscles ache. "Loop, you a washed up junkie. Look at the old sores on your face and shit. Ain't nobody gonna hire you to do shit, but get up out they face. Why put yourself through that?" I get out of bed. "Naw, I say we be who we are, play fast and live hard. We only live once. I loved that feeling you showed me, Loop, and I want it again."

He walks up to me and grabs my shoulders. He is squeezing them so hard that spasms run down my arms and into my elbows. "We fucking done with that shit, do you hear me? I'm gonna get you out of here and we gonna live our lives clean, even if I have to drag you by the hair myself."

He grabs his shoes, and jacket and leaves me in the room alone.

I heard what he said but I'm thinking this. Loop can talk that shit if he wants too, but as soon as I get some money from Cani, to keep his little secret, I'm gonna get another pack. And he gonna thank me for it later too.

CHAPTER 13
Nandi

I'm looking out of my window, when I see Loop bust out of our building's door. He looks angry, like he can commit murder if poked. A boy I saw him talk to in the past, which Jazzy said was a drug dealer, tried to stop him, but he walked right past him like he was a bum begging for change or something.

I never had a problem with Loop before. One time he bought me the dozen powdered donuts from Dunkin's that I like so much, and didn't bother me after I ate them one by one. He sat in my room, and read Cinderella to me three times. It was so much fun.

But now he's hurting my family, and I'm scared. I don't like people who hurt my family. We had too much pain already, and I think we due for some good times. And when I get scared, I get mad. And when I get mad…well…it's not good for anybody.

"Nandi, hey Nandi," someone calls from outside.

When I look down I see Mr. Johnson staring up at me. "How you feeling, girl? You got a smile on your face already, or do you want me to put one on there for you?"

I roll my eyes. "How many you want, Mr. Johnson?"

He's not smiling anymore. He got a serious look on his face now. "Since you don't want to say hi, I'll get right to the point. Which pills you got left?"

I look behind me at the tray. "I got one more Vicodin. You want it?"

"Yeah, give me two."

I pick the bottle up and see only one is left. "I said I ain't got but one, Mr. Johnson. You gonna have to take this and be happy. I'm sorry."

"Well that ain't good enough for me. You know that."

"Well it's gonna have to be," I take the pill out of the bottle and throw it down. He catches it in his mouth, swallows it, and walks away without a thank you or nothing.

I was just about to shut my window when water starts leaking from the ceiling, and falls on my head. First it was a few drops and before I knew it, the roof caves in and everything around me collapses.

CHAPTER 14
Jazzy

"Cani, why are you doing this to me? Is it something I did? I mean, did I do something to make you mad?" I'm holding my cell phone to my ear, standing outside of the Verizon Center, where I have to do the job for Kaitlin. A crowd of people with smiling faces rush past me, as if I'm not even here. Maybe I'm not. This can't be happening…not now. Cani is breaking up with me, and my world is finally caving in around me.

"I'm sorry about this, Jazz, I really am, but I gotta get away for a while. I need some time to think about me and my life, and what I want. At least with us separating for a minute, it will give you some time to focus on your sisters. They need you more than I do."

"That's not true, Cani. Please don't do this to me. I'll do anything you ask me to do, I promise, just don't leave me now. With Love getting high and Nandi tripping too, I can't do this by myself. Come home, and let's talk about how we can make things right, because whatever is wrong I can change. You owe me that at least."

"It's over, Jazz, I'm sorry."

He hangs up on me and I am devastated. My hands drop at my sides and I feel heavy all over. He's not even giving me a reason on why he quit me. I called him earlier today, because yesterday he hadn't called and checked in. Normally I would've called around to try and find him, but I had my hands full with Nandi and Love.

This morning it dawned on me, that I hadn't heard from him when I woke up and I was in the bed alone. So I called him, and he answered but it was like he had an attitude or something. I feel like a zombie right now, and it's hard to even cry anymore.

Part of me wants to go home, and beg him to come over and tell me to my face that he doesn't want me anymore. But Kaitlin is gonna give me the money I need to pay our rent, which is something I don't have. She's more important than him right now.

I take a deep breath, and throw the cell phone in my black book bag. Then I pull out the silver compact mirror, and look at my face, and hair. Kaitlin said Brad liked nerds, so my hair is pulled back into a long black curly ponytail, and I hope this works. I remove the black large rimmed eyeglass frames from my pack, which is held together by a piece of white tape on the left side, a little addition I added to appear more harmless, and less gold-digger-like. I slide them on.

The only makeup I have on is a light pink lipstick—no blush and nothing else. When I'm done, I throw the mirror back in the bag, dust off the plain large red sweatshirt I'm wearing with my tight jeans, and turn around. Taking one last deep breath, I push through the glass doors leading into the Verizon Center. As I'm walking, and I think about what I have to do to get this money, I feel guilty because I'm about to do something mean to a person who doesn't deserve it. Maybe I'm not getting paid enough for this shit, which is something if I do this again, I'll have to think about later.

I'm still feeling bad until my mind moves toward Cyrus, who fucked my sister, got her pregnant, and killed her so she wouldn't take him for child support. If a nigga can fuck a bitch, he can deal with the consequences of his actions if she gets pregnant.

Yeah, this may be wrong, but Brad fucked Kaitlin, and that could have resulted in a pregnancy. The way I look at it, I'm just pushing along the inevitable. Just cause you rich doesn't mean you can do what you want to women. And just because you have a dick doesn't mean you don't have to take care of your children. Fuck niggas! Fuck Cani, and fuck everybody who thinks I'm wrong for wanting to take care of my sisters! I got to get this money.

As I walk inside, I think about Kaitlin's Project, and what the shot will gain her if I am successful, and she get's pregnant.

PROJECT KAITLIN
Name Of Prospect: Brad Simpson
Age: 19
Career: NBA Draft Pick for the Los Angeles Clippers
Future Salary: 5 Million Dollars

If I did this job for Kaitlin, she stood to earn at least a million with his baby alone. Her dollar value would really go up if he is successful on the court of course, and gets with another team.

So I throw the fake Press Pass I made around my neck, and grab my camera, because it's time to get to work. Kaitlin got me tickets on the floor for the Howard Bisons vs. the Georgetown Hoyas basketball game. If Kaitlin is right about him liking nerds, I hope to gain his attention soon.

When I make it to my floor, I show the male attendant my ticket and he winks at me and lets me inside. I go straight down, take my seat and wait for the game to start. Thirty minutes later the players run out and I get a look at number 22. He's tall, which considering the game he plays isn't so special, but he's also very attractive. His hair is the color of a paper bag, and his light skin glows under the center's lights. It definitely looks like he takes care of himself.

Before long the game is under way and I talk myself out of leaving five times. Just thinking about Nandi not being able to breathe, or us being thrown out on the street is enough to make me push forward.

Before long the first quarter ends, and although I get a few looks from the other players on both teams, I still don't get what I wanted from Brad. It was time to turn the nerdy look down just a little, and turn up the sex appeal. So I remove my red sweatshirt, revealing a white wifebeater underneath. My breasts although small, spill out at the top. And I adjust the press pass so that it falls within my cleavage, and pick up my camera.

Now I can feel the eyes on me from behind, and when I look out onto the court, Brad is staring at me. I smile shyly, look down at my camera and snap a few pics like I'm not interested. For the rest of the game, whenever Brad gets a break, he uses it to stare into my face.

When the game is over, I pretend like my work is done, and I'm about to leave. That is until someone jumps in from of me, and steps on my brand new Jordan's.

"I'm sorry, ma," the husky man says to me, "but Brad Simpson is interested in you. I wanted to catch you before you left."

"So you step on my shoes?"

He looks down at them, bends down and slaps the dust away from my sneakers, as if my comment is dumb. He's heavy handed so the shit hurts my big toes, and I contemplate kicking him. Looking back at me he says, "Is that better?"

"I guess," I say rolling my eyes.

"Good, because the last thing you gonna be worried about in a minute are your sneaks. Like I said, my man is trying to get your attention." He points at the court but I don't look.

"I don't know no Brad," I say walking around him.

"Wait," he says grabbing my arm a little too forcefully. "Now I don't know if you realize it or not, but Brad is gonna be drafted this year into the NBA, hopefully the Clippers, which will make him a millionaire. Now you cute, a little too square for my taste, but Brad thinks you fine. Now unless you got millionaires approaching you all the time, I suggest you drop the fucking attitude and follow me. Right this way."

I'm so mad I say, "Fuck off you ugly-monkey-dog," and walk away from him.

Upscale KITTENS

If I gotta go through all of this shit I'm not interested. *Fuck Brad. Fuck Big Husky and Fuck Kaitlin.* I snatch the press pass off of my neck, and move toward the door until I hear sneakers running behind me. Scared it's Big Husky again, I turn around and see who's coming. I'm now staring up into the face of Brad Simpson, a possible first round draft pick, and Kaitlin's project.

"Where you going, beautiful," he asks grabbing my arm again.

What's up with athletes these days? They're so fucking arrogant and aggressive, and I can't stand them. "Home," I say snatching from him.

"Well can I go home with you?"

"Is that one of your tired ass lines or something," I ask. "Because if it is I have heard better. Now if you will excuse me, I have some place to be." I turn around again and move for the exit. I'll explain to my homie later that this thing was an epic fail.

"Look, I'm sorry if my man came at you the wrong way," he says. "I don't have this star shit down yet, but I'm a really good person. Sometimes I be thinking that women like dudes to come at them hard, because it makes them feel special. I can see now that I'm wrong about you. Now all I want to do is invite you back to the suite, have a few drinks and get to know you a little better."

I turn around to look at him. "I'm not fucking you, if that's on your mind."

"It's not even like that," he says holding his hands up. "Just some conversation and drinks?" I pout. "Come on, what do you say, maybe we can start all over."

by Candee

Got him.

I'm in the Presidential Suites with him and we are alone. I've had two drinks already and he has had a whole bottle. I can see why Kaitlin likes him. Outside of him being an athlete, he really seems like a good person and I like that about him. For instance he asked me about my day, and I was tempted to tell him until I remembered I'm a liar and he is my job, not my friend.

After he showered and came out of his uniform, he seemed humble but I know in about two years, I won't recognize him anymore. He'll be just as arrogant and mean as the rest of the NBA players, once that money taps his pockets, the way he was when we first met. And that alone makes me feel justified in what I'm about to do.

I sit on the sofa and he sits next to me. "So, what are you gonna get into tonight," I ask him trying to appear as meek as possible.

"You, if you let me," he says. He wipes his head with the white rag that is hanging over his shoulder, and places it in his lap.

I adjust my fake glasses. "That's rude. You shouldn't talk to girls like that."

"I didn't mean it like that, but them glasses with the tape on the sides, and your jeans with the sneakers on is just too cute. I don't know what it is, but there's something about a smart girl that I just fuck with."

"You mean a smart nerd."

"Naw, I mean smart girl. I mean what I say and say what I mean, Jordan." Jordan is the fake name I gave him. "You beautiful, and I can tell you're not trying to be on purpose. I hate bitches like that, all made up and wanting a nigga to see them, and make them wifey. Like that will be enough to get the ring. You came to the game to do your job, and you wasn't tripping off of none of the players on the court."

You're right about that, I had my eye on you.

He takes the tie out of my ponytail, and my long hair cascades down my arms and back. "You're stunning, Jordan." He runs his thumb across my lips. *So gross.* "In a natural kind of way."

I look down into my lap and say, "Thank you. I think."

When I look up, he is naked from the waist down, staring at me. Since he had a bottle of wine by himself I knew he was buzzing, but didn't think he was this far-gone.

"Come over here," he says stroking his long thick dick, "come taste it for me, Jordan. Put them pretty pink lips right here, where they belong, on the eye hole of my fish."

Ugh. Just looking at him makes me disgusted. I gotta try to find away to do this job, without throwing up, but I know it's gonna be hard. So I close my eyes, and pull up in my mind my troubles. Nandi is sick in the head and body. Love is a heroin addict, and I'm all they got in the world. I exhale, and open my eyes, preparing to get down to business.

"I never done this before," I say looking at his weapon, also known as a dick.

He smirks. "Yeah right, now stop fucking around and come over here. I want you to kiss it for me."

"I don't want to," I shake my head. "This is not me, Brad."

"I know, that's why I want you. And trust me, whatever we do here stays here. You don't have to worry about me telling my teammates or no shit like that. This is between me and you."

"You promise?"

He removes his hand from his dick and crosses his heart. "I promise."

I move closer to him, ease between his legs and drop to my knees. His head is leaning back, so he doesn't see me take the plastic saran wrap out of my back pocket and place it on the floor at his feet.

I guess I'm not moving fast enough because he says, "Come on now. What are you waiting on?" He looks me in the eyes. "I'm ready for you to suck this dick until it's flat."

"Can I wipe it first?"

"Either you suck my dick or get the fuck out of my suite," he yells. "I'm Brad Simpson, and I got about fifty bitches in the stadium that would love to be in your shoes right now. Consider yourself lucky. You played the game and it worked, and now you back here with me. So stop fucking around."

I guess the Mr. Nice Guy movie is over. "That's all you got wanting to take my place? 50?"

"You gonna do it or not," he asks.

"I'll do it," I say trying to hold my food in from earlier today, "I'll do it." *Please Kaitlin take this nigga to the cleaners.*

"Then hurry the fuck up," he says before dropping his head backwards again, and closing his eyes.

I take his dick into my hands and I feel my stomach juices swirl. My jaw feels warm, and I can feel acids from my stomach splashing into my throat. I close my eyes, lower my neck and take him into my mouth. In seconds my food doesn't hold and I throw up on his penis and look up at him. I just know he's about to throw me out but he doesn't seem to notice.

"Yeah, just like that, make it wet baby," he says to me. "Real wet."

I allow my throw up to spill over his dick, and move the plastic out of the way so it doesn't get on it. And then I think about Cani, and how much I love him. I think about all the nights he sang to my sister, and how much he loves me. I tell myself that this is Cani, and that he broke up with me, and that this is what he wants me to do before he takes me back. For some reason, as dirty as the situation is now, I don't care anymore. I am somewhere else mentally.

When I hear Brad moaning a lot, I figure I'm doing a good job because he's responding by pumping into my face. I raise my head, wipe his dick off with the rag and go back to work.

"Stop fucking around," he says looking down at me. "I'm about to cum." He drops his head back and I get back to work. *Asshole.*

I'm glad I wiped it, because if he's about to cum, I need his dick as clean as possible for Kaitlin's shot. When I feel the veins on his dick pulsating in my mouth, I know what's about to happen, so I raise my head, jerk him hard and grip my plastic. I look up at him, and his head is still back, as cum shoots out of his dick and into the plastic, I smile. When I'm done I ball it up real quickly, stuff it into my back pocket, and place my mouth back on his dick again. I wasn't timing it but if I had to, I'd say it took me less than fifteen seconds.

He's still moaning when he looks down at me, and I'm still licking his dick like it's candy. "Damn, girl, you swallowed?"

I nod and wipe the corners of my mouth. "Yep.

"I knew there was a reason I liked you."

"I guess you know how to pick them. I do too."

Sperm can live outside of the body if it remains wet for hours. But after it dries forget about it, it's worthless, and can't get anybody pregnant. So Kaitlin knew she only had a few minutes to place it in her body, so I caught a cab to her house after she promised to pay for it.

The moment I walked inside her apartment, she grabbed the plastic ball out of my hand, and went into the bathroom with a turkey baster from her kitchen. When she was finished doing her thing, she rushed back out into the living room with me.

"Girl, you hooked me up," she says hugging me, with the creamy baster still in her hands.

"You wanna throw that in the kitchen or some-thing," I say, knowing it had been in her pussy.

"Oh I'm sorry, girl," she laughs throwing the baster in the kitchen sink. *Gross.* "Come with me over on the couch, Jazzy, I have to sit on my head to make sure it works. So the cum can go straight to my ovaries. If this doesn't work I'm not gonna get another chance."

"If you say so," I laugh.

When we get to the couch, she sits on her head, with her feet in the air. This girl is so crazy. "So what did you have to do to get it?" She looks over at me. "And what's up with the glasses?"

I take them off. "These glasses are what helped me get his attention," I throw them into my book bag. "And it was easier than you realize to get the shot for you."

"But how," she asks, as I walk into the kitchen to grab a Coke. "He was so serious about protecting his sperm, that he didn't wanna have nothing else to do with me unless we wore five condoms."

"That's because you were pressing the issue about having sex with him, and I avoided the topic all togeth-er. I acted like I was a virgin and sex was the plague. It ended up with me sucking his dick, and giving you what you needed." She seems sad. "I hope you didn't mind, since you put me on him."

"Naw, it hurts to hear it a little, because at one point I thought he was the one, but it didn't work out like that." She sighs. "Wait." Her eyes widen. "Did you say you sucked a dick? What you make him do, wash it in bleach first?"

"I wanted to."

She laughs and sits on her butt instead. "Jazzy Law, you never cease to amaze me." She shakes her head again. "Anyway, what are you gonna do for a new place now? Because I'd let you stay here, but you know I got a roommate too, which is why I needed that shot you just gave me. A dose of that nigga's juice will set me up for life once he makes it to the NBA."

I frown. "What you mean what am I gonna do for a new place?"

She leans in. "Wait…Love didn't tell you?"

"Tell me what?"

She pulls me toward her. "Oh, girl, I'm so sorry I gotta be the one to tell you this shit. The ceiling came down at your apartment today, in Nandi's room. They condemned your place and everything."

"Where is Nandi?" I yell.

"You gotta ask Love."

CHAPTER 15
Jazzy

"Love, why the fuck didn't you tell me that the ceiling came in on Nandi," I yell. She's standing in the middle of the living room, looking stupid as usual, and I'm sitting on the sofa. I'm not sure, but I think she's been using again because her eyes are lazy. "You didn't hit my cell phone or nothing. What if Nandi got hurt?"

"She didn't."

Last night was terrible. The apartment was so cold, because although Nandi's bedroom door was shut, there was a gaping hole where the window use to be, and if you looked up, you could see the bathroom sink. Apparently Trudy from upstairs, fell asleep after a long night of drinking, and forgot she left the bath water running in the tub. Her weak ass floor came in on our ceiling.

Nandi and I had to sleep in the living room, and I was up all night dealing with her nightmares and crying. Love left her here by herself, and she didn't bring her ass into the house until just now.

"I'm gonna leave ya'll to it," Loop says, kissing Love on the cheek. Although I'm not a fan, he did help me try to find her last night, even though we were unsuccessful. "I'll be back later."

"No you won't," I tell him. "You not allowed back in my home, Loop. I told you that. The reason she doing all this extra shit is because of you."

"Either he stays or I go," Love tells me. "If you want me to go out there in them streets, and have something happen to me, like what happened to Angela, you tell him he can't come back here anymore, and see what happens. You will never see me again, Jazzy. Never!"

I think about what the doctor says about her being suicidal and I hang my head low. I'm tempted to take her up on her offer, and throw her out onto the streets, but I don't have the heart. If something else happened to her I would be dead.

I look up at him. "Can you please leave us alone for a minute, Loop? Please." He walks out. When the door closes I look at Love. "Why do you hate me so much? I mean, I know I wasn't the best person in the world. And, I know I made some mistakes, and a lot of them at that, but I'm doing all that I can to make things right with you now. And to keep our family together."

"You sound dumb."

"I'm serious," I yell. "I don't know if you are aware but I just lost my job, and had to do something I will never tell another person but Kaitlin, just to pay the rent. But, it doesn't matter to me because the only thing on my mind is keeping my family together. And by family I mean you, Nandi and me. Cani dumped me so we are through. We really are all that we got."

She looks like she's smiling from the news that me and Cani are over.

"What can I do to make things right with you? I don't know what it is so you gotta tell me."

Upscale KITTENS

Her jaw looks so tight I am afraid her teeth are going to break. "It's because of you he hurt me," she says. "All of this is your fault, and your karma."

"Mine," I point to myself. "What do you mean? I was a victim too."

"You know exactly what the fuck I mean."

I'm twisting and snaking in my seat. "Stop being mean to Jazzy, Love," Nandi says from behind me, "I don't like when you're mean to her. I told you that."

"Nandi, it's okay," I say to her, "Love is just upset right now. Come sit next to me." She sits on the far end of the sofa, away from me. Times like this I would send her to her room, but she no longer has one.

"Fuck upset, I'm angry," she screams, causing my heart to stop. "You let him hurt me, you let him come into my room all those nights because you, and I quote, *'couldn't take it anymore'*. You didn't care about what he would do to me, or what he would do to Nandi. You were older, and you were supposed to protect us. But all you wanted to do was protect yourself. Isn't that right?"

"W-what do you mean," I stutter, "he never bothered you, h-he, never…"

"How the fuck would you know," Love says wiping her tears away, leaving wet streaks down her cheeks. "After Angie did her job, you were supposed to do yours, and fuck him, suck him, or whatever else he asked you to do as long as he stayed away from us. But because you couldn't take it anymore, he entered our room and made me do…he made me…"

My blood is raging. I knew what Cyrus did to Angela and me. But I never thought my sisters had to go

115

through the same things too. I look over at Nandi. "Did Cyrus ever touch you?" I really don't want to know but I ask anyway.

She turns away from me, and I move closer to her. I gently move her chin, so that we can look into each other's eyes. "Nandi, did he ever hurt you?"

"Only on the days you couldn't take it no more."

I throw my face into my hands and sob long and hard. I never meant for my sisters to be involved in anything regarding Cyrus. I did everything he asked me to do, even some things I never knew were possible. But, sometimes his rapes hurt so much that it was blinding and along with a good fight, I begged him to stop and some days he left me alone. He would just leave my room, and I never knew before now where he went. I guess I didn't care, or didn't want to know.

"I'm sorry, Love, I didn't know."

"You knew, Jazzy," she gives me a smile that is all lip and no teeth. "You knew exactly what was going on. The day it all started, he walked out of your bedroom, and he turned the knob leading into me and Nandi's room. I saw you standing there, and softly begged you to make him go away. But what did you do?

"I don't remember."

"Yes you do," she screams. "You closed the door, Jazz. You closed the door, and now I'm fucked up for the rest of my life. And then you want to take away Loop? What about Nandi is killing again? You know she is, and I know she is, the only question is what are we going to do to get it to stop this time?"

"Nandi, isn't killing again," I tell her, although I know the truth. "That stopped a long time ago." I look at Nandi. "Right?"

"Nandi is killing again, Jazzy. And unless you get her the help she needs, its gonna get worse before it gets better. Instead of worrying about who I'm fucking, or what I'm sticking into my arms, you need to give that shit the attention it needs."

"Jazzy, there's nothing I can do about it," Martin Rover says to me. He's a beastly man, with a hairy face – gray hair, thick eyebrows and a moustache that ran into his unruly beard. Martin is the property manager, and a complete asshole. The only thing he cares about is the rent, and golf. He could give a fuck about his tenants or repairs.

"But, I need a place to live," I beg him. "I mean what about my sisters? Nandi has asthma and needs a breathing machine."

"Jazzy, we do not have any more three bedroom apartments available," he grabs one of the clubs out of the golf bag, and walks over to the small putting green in the middle of his office. He doesn't have a care in the world. "You're gonna have to make other arrangements, because I can't help you right now." He stands behind the ball, taps it, and misses his mark when the ball rolls under his desk.

"But this isn't fair," I yell at him, as he sits behind his large wooden desk, "it is not our fault that the ceiling came crashing down on my sister's head."

"And it's not our fault either, Jazzy. It's called an act of nature, look it up. The weather banged against the building and brought it down. What do you want me to do?"

"But it wasn't raining or snowing when it happened, Martin."

"How would you know? Didn't you, and that newly addicted drug addict sister of yours, leave Nandi in the apartment all by herself?" My eyes widen. "Oh I know a lot of shit that goes on around here. Between Mr. Johnson and the CD man, folks talk in this building, believe that. As far as I'm concerned you can't say shit to me about what happened when the ceiling came down, because you weren't there."

I hate him so much right now, but I'm willing to do anything to keep my family together. And, I do mean anything.

"Can you at least give us another apartment to stay in, until the apartment is repaired?"

"The only apartment we have is $700 a month, and you can barely pay the rent on the $500 a month one you have now. I mean look how late you gave me the $500.00." he taps my rent on his desk "I didn't even charge you the late fee, but don't nobody care about that."

"We'll take it," I yell. "The $700.00 apartment."

He laughs, and leans back into his seat, and it squeaks. "Jazzy, you are delusional."

"I need some place to stay."

"And like I said the last few times," he smirks, "I can't help you."

"Then I want to speak to Killion," I yell at him.

He isn't smiling anymore. "Jazzy Law, now do you really want to speak to that nigga? Because unlike me, he's not gonna be as nice to you as I am. He got another way to deal with bothersome niggas like you. Is that what you really want?"

by Candee

CHAPTER 16
Love
(2 WEEKS LATER)

I've been having a hard time lately. Since Loop has made a decision to stay clean, I have to cop from Brandon, and get high alone. Because Cani is not around anymore, I had to do other things to get money. Brandon had me doing all kind of freaked out shit, but I'll do anything for my next hit. It's just that simple.

The other day he made me bend over in the alley, while he took pictures of my naked ass and pussy with his iPhone. Then he gave me a hit, and made me piss in the corner while he videotaped it. I can only imagine where that footage will end up. And then there's the fact that I don't care.

As much as I shoot up, I'm noticing that it isn't the same since Loop decided to clean up his life. All he wanted to do these days was look for a job, to try to get us an apartment. I don't want another apartment; I want him to come back to the world he dropped me off at. And the past few days he's been out, and when he comes back he smells of liquor and sex. I don't even want to know what he does, because then I'll be forced to do something about him cheating when for real I'm not worried. I'm so confused.

And then we are living some place that is temporary. Jazzy was able to convince the property manager to give us this apartment for two weeks, but he swore if we didn't have the money by Saturday, we would be out on the streets. I don't know what she had to do, but I do know she was in his office for an hour after he said no within the first fifteen minutes of her visit. So I forged my own conclusions. She fucked him to set things right.

Although this place is much better than the one that's condemned, I know there is no use in us getting comfortable. With Cani gone, and me not working, Jazzy can't afford this place on her own, and sometimes I wonder why I care. Jazzy ruined my life when I was a kid, and I blame her for everything. Sometimes when I go to sleep, I pray that she has eternal damnation in hell.

The moment I open the door to my room, to walk into the living room, I'm struck in the head with something long and silver. When I fall to the floor, and try to protect my face, I am hit repeatedly and the pain burns. Through the blood running down my forehead I see Nandi's face.

"Nandi, what the fuck are you doing," I yell, grabbing at the long silver object in her hands, which is threatening to take my life. When I finally have my fingers around it, I can see it's a golf club. Where did she get this from? After I have it out of her hand, I toss it toward the kitchen, out of her reach. It bangs against the refrigerator.

"You shouldn't be mad with Jazzy, you shouldn't be mad with Jazzy," Nandi screams at me over and over again.

I finally get a hold of her body, by sitting on the wall in the living room, with her stuffed between my thighs. My arms and legs are wrapped around her body, and I'm controlling her blows this way.

"Get off of me," she yells, trying to wiggle out of my grasp, "I hate you so much!"

I rock her in my arms. "Nandi, it's okay. Don't worry, things will be okay. I have you, and nobody is going to bother you again."

"I hate you," she continues yelling as I rock her harder. "Why you gotta make me hit you? Why you make me do that to your head?"

Poor Nandi. I knew this was gonna happen again sooner or later, but I always assumed we would have more time. After Angela was murdered, and we were stuffed into the freezer for protection, Nandi became a little monster. It all started six months after Angela's death, but I swear as long as I have a memory, I'll never forget the day her personality changed. Even though I try.

● ● ● ● ● ● ● ● ●

6 YEARS EARLIER
Blooming Flowers Group Home

"Let me get something straight, at Blooming Flowers Group Home, I am God," Mrs. Bickers said to the Law sisters, as they stood near the foyer, with their luggage at their feet. "If anything goes on in my house,"

she pulls on the brown cigarette between her lips, "anywhere in this facility at all, I will know about it and I will bring down the wrath like no other," she smirked, waving the long black leather strap in her other hand to express her power. "Now the three of you go outside in the back, and shake your clothes out before we put a thing upstairs. I don't want roaches in my home, because around here we are insect free." The sisters trotted upstairs, past the gray lion sculpture made of stone.

That was just the beginning of Mrs. Bicker's crossness. Whenever the sisters would cry over the loss of their oldest sister, she would come down over their backs with her leather rod, ripping into their skin. If there was one thing she hated, weakness was it.

Mrs. Bickers was evil reincarnated. The only reason she applied for the job was so she could rule over young women, like her mean grandmother terrorized her life as a teenager, after her mother died. The only thing that kept Mrs. Bickers calm was her chain-smoking habit, but once the last pull was drawn, she was back to her evil games.

Things turned worse when one day the girls were sitting at the long wooden dining room table, with bowls of disgusting oatmeal in front of them. Nandi was quietly sobbing on Jazzy's shoulder, as she continued to recall the memory of her mother's frozen corpse, and the blood on the floor from Angela's body, as she exited the freezer. No matter how hard Nandi tried, she could not shake either memory from her mind.

"You gotta keep your voice down," Love whispered rubbing Nandi's back softly. It was Saturday, and the

123

other members of the group home were sleep, which was how the Law sisters liked it, so they got up early. "If Mrs. Bickers gets up, and hears you crying again, she's gonna hurt us. You don't want that do you?"

"She can't help her feelings," Jazzy told her, "we are fucked up by what happened to Angela, Love. But she's younger, so she's taking it a little harder that's all."

"You not more fucked up than I am," Love combatted, "you could never be more fucked up. Ever!"

The increase in Love's voice caused Mrs. Bickers to roll out of her bed and come charging down the stairs, with the leather rod in hand. Without asking questions, and because she was awaken prematurely, she grabbed Jazzy's hair and slapped her across the face with the switch causing her skin to open.

"No," Nandi screamed, slapping Mrs. Bickers all over the back with both hands, "stop hurting my sister!"

"Get off of me, you ungrateful little bitch," Mrs. Bickers yelled, turning her attention toward Nandi. "I'll teach you how to show adults respect."

After quite a fight, Jazzy and Love were able to free Nandi, and Nandi dashed upstairs. Mrs. Bickers caught up with Jazzy and Love at the foyer, and slapped them everywhere her switch would land. She grabbed Jazzy by the hair, preparing to hit her again when Nandi dropped the ugly lion sculpture over the banister. It fell on the top of Mrs. Bickers' head and knocked her out cold.

"Oh my, God," Love said covering her mouth, and looking up at Nandi who was smiling brightly. "What did you do?"

"She wouldn't stop," Nandi replied. "So I had to make her."

"Forget all of that, let's pull her into our room, so we can figure out what we gonna do now," Jazzy directed.

They kept her in the room for six hours. When the other girls woke up in the home, the Law sisters moved about the house normally, pretending as if nothing was going on. And when the children asked where Mrs. Bickers and the lion sculpture went, the Law sisters faked dumb.

Later that night Mrs. Bickers had awaken, and with a weak-low voice, threatened to tell the police if they didn't release her immediately. Her threats held little weight, because she could not move, or speak to anyone unless they put a phone to her ear. Due to the sculpture being dropped on her head, she was paralyzed from the neck down. The blow Nandi gave her was severe and precise. She needed help and she needed it immediately if she were going to survive.

The three of them were in the room looking at her, when Jazzy said, "Love, let me talk to you for a minute," she looked at Nandi, "out in the hallway."

Love and Jazzy stepped outside of the room to discuss some ways to handle the problem without being caught, and separated. At first Jazzy was going to take the rap, but Love begged her not too. They ran a few ideas over in their heads, but when they came back into

by Candee

the room they realized it didn't matter. Nandi was holding a pillow over Mrs. Bicker's face, and pressing down
hard. And because Mrs. Bickers was paralyzed, she
could not defend herself.

Jazzy and Love rushed toward their sister, and removed her from Mrs. Bickers body, but it was too late.
The moment Jazzy placed a finger to the vein on her
neck, she knew it was over, her blood was not coursing,
and Mrs. Bickers was gone. She was dead.

Later that night when all the kids were asleep, they
placed Mrs. Bickers face down in her own bed, with a
cigarette in one hand and a glass of bourbon in the other. The scene would say that the cigarette mysteriously
fell out of Mrs. Bicker's grasp, and lit the room on fire.

While the room was going up in flames the Law sisters, were outside the door, watching. They remained
quiet, until they saw the smoke crawl from the bottom of
the door, and move into the house. They figured at that
point Mrs. Bickers should be burned enough to cover
Nandi's crime, and the broke lion's sculpture went out
with the day's trash. With everything in place Jazzy
yelled, 'FIRE, FIRE, FIRE,' into the house, alerting
everyone else.

The crime was investigated briefly, but the world
knew about Mrs. Bicker's cigarette habit, and some said
it was karma for her evil ways.

When they were in the next home, and safe from
Mrs. Bicker's antics, Jazzy and Love sat Nandi down
and made her swear to never do anything as vile again.
They were afraid that if someone found out, she would
be locked away, and never returned to her family.

Upscale KITTENS

Nandi promised, sure enough, to never kill again, but it wasn't long before they realized it was all a lie.

"I'm sorry, Love," Nandi says crying in my arms, "I didn't mean to hurt you, I just don't want you to fight Jazzy no more."

"I know, I know," I reply rubbing the back of her head, trying to ignore my own pain. "We gonna get you some help, don't worry. We gonna get you a lot of help too."

"Don't let them take me away," she cries, "I'll be good if you don't let them take me."

"Nobody is taking you anywhere, I promise."

"Nandi, you know we gotta pay more money if we want to keep this apartment," Jazzy says walking into my room.

The wound Nandi caused to my head is on the other side of my face. Jazzy would have to be standing in front of me to see it, and I'm relieved. I don't want to tell her about the bruise because after a few other things happened in the past, Jazzy contemplated having Nandi committed. And, I don't want my baby sister in no crazy home, just because Princess Jazzy can't take it anymore.

"And," I say shrugging.

She rolls her eyes, "And, we don't have the money, but Kaitlin called earlier and said she has another job for me."

"If by job you're talking about the little sperm bank thing you got going on, I'm not interested. Leave me out of it." I try to forget about what I did for Brandon, because in my mind it doesn't matter and she doesn't know about it. I hate being a hypocrite.

"Love, I know you might not like what I had to do, but I told you because I wanted to be honest, and I don't want us having secrets. Now Kaitlin called earlier today and told me she's pregnant. That means she's gonna make a lot of paper from Brad the moment she has that baby. When she said that, I told her to put the word out about my skills, and she got me another gig. But the person who wants my help now, needs somebody who looks like you. And I need you to step up and help me out, Love. I'll tell you everything that you need to do."

"Jazzy, I don't..."

"Please," she says crying, "I feel like I'm on my own around here. I feel like nobody is helping me. All I want you to do is meet with this client, and see if it's something you can help me with. Okay?"

"Who's the prospect?"

"Killion...the nigga who owns this building."

CHAPTER 17
Love

I'm sitting on the edge of the bed, trying to think about my next move. My toes are flat against the wooden floor, and I realize they are colorless. Since my first bout with heroin, I've been constantly falling off, and don't even do stuff I use to like get my nails polished. But, unlike Loop, I don't want to stop the drugs or give up how they make me feel. I like not thinking about life. I like not having to remember the past, and I like not having to deal with the fact that our baby sister Nandi, is a certified killer. I just wish he felt the same way about getting high, maybe I should tell him about my crazy sister and he'll feel sorry for me.

"Love, what the fuck is going on around here," Loop asks coming into my room, "what happened to your head, and why is Nandi in her room crying, and asking somebody not to take her away?"

"It's a long story," I tell him.

"Don't tell me that shit, what happened?"

"I fell getting out of the tub," I lie.

"Love, let's get out of this house. I don't like what's going on around here anymore. You and your sister argue like you're enemies and it's not healthy. I've been looking around for some places..."

"You can't afford to take care of me, Loop," I yell at him. "So stop fooling yourself."

He digs into his pocket and pulls out a stack of money, the outside of the mound is covered with one hundred dollar bills, so I could only imagine what bills were in the middle. My eyes bubble and my pussy gets wets.

Holding it firmly in his hand he says, "Never underestimate the mind of a determined man." He steps closer, drops on his knee and grabs my hands. "Love, let me take care of you the way I know I can." He throws the money into my lap. "That is our money, about $4,000 to start all over, and it's all ours."

My eyes widen and I grab the green stack, and smile. With $4,000 I could get high all day long. But, it's not the same if Loop is not with me. I have to find away to get him trapped again. I have to find a way to bring him back into the Heroin World he left me in. He's gonna do it anyway, heroin addicts always fall back if they don't get help, at least that's what I heard anyway.

"So what do you say, baby? You gonna let me take you out of here, and start all over, like I always wanted to do for you, before I got sick?"

"Where did you get the money," I ask, holding the stash. "I had a job for years and never seen this amount of money in my life."

"It doesn't matter, baby, all that matters is that I have it, and this money is enough to give us another chance. I'm applying for an apartment out Maryland, the new development called Hills Plaza."

"Killion's property?"

"Yes, but it's one of his better ones. I talked to the property manager and it looks like everything is going to be okay, and we can move out the moment we ready. You see, Love, the only thing I'm waiting on is you."

"If I say yes, will you do one last hit with me?"

He stands up and walks toward the wall. "Babes, I can't do that shit no more, aren't you listening to me? I watched what it did to you and it changed my life. Do you know how I felt seeing you like that, knowing there was nothing I could do to help you? I'm never fucking with that shit again, Love. I'm sorry."

He sounds like a nerd. Like a square. "But what about me? I don't want to stop, and it's unfair for you to make me do the shit by myself."

He walks over to me, bends down and grabs both of my arms. "Love, you better not be fucking around with that shit no more. Are you?"

I don't respond. Instead I get up and walk toward the mirror to brush my hair. "I don't want to stop the feeling, Loop." I place the money on the dresser. "And I don't want you to stop either. If you love me as much as you say you do, you'll understand that. When you wanted to get high, I didn't abandon you, or look down on you. I did what you did because I loved you that much."

From the mirror I see a tear fall from his face, but he quickly wipes it away. "I'm sorry, Love, I really am...I just...I just..."

"Don't love me enough to take the trip back to the other side? Even though I need you? Even though I don't want to be alone?"

"I gotta go," he walks toward the door, "I'm sorry, baby, I just can't." He left the room, leaving the money behind.

131

As he was walking out of the apartment Jazzy, was walking into my bedroom. "I just got off of the phone with Kaitlin, Aphrodite is coming over here tonight. If this works out, and we can get the shot she needs, we'll have a thousand dollars, which is enough money to rent this apartment and get Nandi what she needs." She steps further into the room and looks at my face. "What happened to your head?"

"What do you think?" I place my hand over the money to hide it.

She backs up and covers her mouth. "Nandi?"

"I'm gonna have to get her some help, Love."

"Tell me something I don't know already."

"I'm talking about institutional help."

I rush toward her and get up in her face. We are so close our breasts touch. "Bitch, if you put Nandi away I will kill you. In all of her fucked-up-ness, remember that this is your fault. And you can't abandon her away, just because you don't feel like dealing with it no more."

She wipes her hands down her face. And with an attitude she says, "Get yourself together, Love. Aphrodite will be here in an hour. Lets see what she has to say." She walks out of the door, and leaves me alone.

Sure I could've given her some of the money for the rent, but it doesn't belong to her. Truthfully it doesn't belong to Loop either, after all, I spent a lot of money on him when he use to get high and live in our basement. It's payback. This money is going to buy me enough dope to set me up for at least a week, and it's the only thing on my mind right now.

CHAPTER 18
Jazzy

Me and Love are sitting at our kitchen table across from Aphrodite. She's a pretty girl, who looks mixed with black and some other nationality that I can't place my finger on. She has long cascading blonde hair, but her skin is as brown as honey. She looks almost foreign, and I wonder what caused her to hitch her star to Killion, when she could get anybody to take care of her. Who would be glad to have a child with her.

"I really appreciate you doing this for me," Aphrodite says to me. "Kaitlin is a good friend of mine, and when she told me what you did for her, I knew you could probably help me. Before this, I didn't think it was even possible."

"We haven't agreed to do shit yet," Love says sitting back in the seat.

"What my sister means is that we have to go over some details first, if we are going to get involved. It's for your safety and ours."

"No, what I mean is exactly what I said. Kaitlin was out of order for telling you what my sister did for her. That's not exactly the kind of shit that needs to be advertised around DC."

"I know, but Kaitlin says she asked Jazzy if she could tell me first," she says in a low voice. "I know Kaitlin not broadcasting the news to anyone but me."

"That's true," I say, "she asked me and I said it was cool to tell you."

"Great," she smiles, "and all I'm saying is that I appreciate it. Kaitlin even told me how to check my ovulation cycle and I've been doing it already. As a matter of fact, I'm high now so I should be ovulating within the next four days. So it's important that if you're going to help me, that we do it now."

"Tell me about Killion," I say, "I mean, the most we know about him is that—"

"He's a fucking slum lord who doesn't take care of his properties, and who almost killed my sister by having a faulty roof when it caved in on her head," Love says interrupting me. "That's enough for me not to like him."

"Yes, he's not the best person in the world, but he is rich," Aphrodite responds.

"How rich?"

PROJECT APHRODITE
Name Of Prospect: Killion Holmes
Age: 25
Career: Drug Kingpin, Real Estate Mogul, Owner of The Right Fit tennis shoes chain
Net Worth: 23 Million Dollars

After she gave us his financial background, about the buildings, the stores and the money, I could see why she would want to have a baby by him. Shit, I wanted to have a baby by him now. Unlike with Brad Simpson, the basketball player, one baby by Killion could make Aphrodite a millionaire for life, because outside of dealing dope, he was also a businessman, which meant he knew what to do with his money.

"Sounds like your boy is paid, so why can't you get the shot yourself," Love asks. "I mean you are fucking him right?"

"He broke up with me some weeks ago," she says hanging her head low. A tear falls out of her eyes and onto my table. "He told me he didn't love me anymore, and that he was done. I feel like I wasted my life on him for nothing. Killion is a real jealous man, and he took all of my time without giving me an allowance or a hope for a future without him. Now he dumped me and I'm broke. I figured if I have this baby, not only will he realize how much he loves me, but he'll be able to take care of me."

"Having niggas' babies don't mean you gonna be set for life," Love says. "My sister was nine months pregnant when the nigga who knocked her up killed her. You better be sure Killion don't do the same thing to you, if this shit works. I'm just letting you know."

Aphrodite's eyes widen. "I'm sorry to hear that...I mean....about your sister."

I'm so mad at Love right now. It's like she's trying to sabotage this job on purpose. If she doesn't want to do it, she should just say that, instead of trying to fuck things up when she knows we need this money. I'm starting to lose my patience where Love is concerned.

"It's cool, Aphrodite," I tell her. "There is no amount of apologies that will take away our pain, or bring my sister back anyway. But listen, I want to help you, but you have to tell me more about Killion in terms of what kind of women he likes."

She looks me over, and then she looks over Love. "She'll definitely be his type. I've seen him pick out girls to join him in VIP before, at Club Vixen that I told you about. If you send her in, she'll be the one he chooses. Will you help me?" She looks at Love.

Love doesn't respond, instead she gets up, walks to the refrigerator and grabs a beer.

"Love, are you gonna do it or not," I yell at her.

"You shouldn't do stuff like that," Nandi says from the doorway. "You remember what happened to Angie. What if the man finds out what you did and tries to kill you? Like Cyrus did Angie."

"Nandi, go back into your room," I yell at her. When she doesn't move I say, "Now!"

Nandi rolls her eyes, looks at Aphrodite and leaves.

I focus back on Love, because we are still waiting for an answer.

"What you gonna do, Love?"

"I'll do it."

"Oh my, God," Aphrodite says clapping her hands, "I so appreciate this."

"Before we go too far, let me make some things clear," I tell her. "Killion can never find out that we helped you. Ever! If he does, and I do mean this, I will find you. And when I find you it won't be nice, because I don't play when it comes to my family."

"Jazzy, I would never do anything to hurt you or your family. Trust me, your secret is safe with me. Besides, you're hooking me up. Why would I mess this up? I would never want anybody to know how I really got pregnant." She pauses. "I understand that you want a thousand dollars right? I'll give it to you when I receive the shot."

"Yes."

"Okay, well when can we start," Aphrodite asks.

"Well when do you expect he will be at Club Vixen again?"

"Tomorrow."

"Then we'll start right away," I say.

by Candee

CHAPTER 19
Love

I'm in the club, with a slight buzz, looking at Killion across the room. It's funny, I haven't been this close to him ever. Normally when I see him, he's driving past the front of our apartment building in his shiny black Mercedes, even though the toilets in his properties don't flush, and the heater never works. But there he is, throwing our money up in the air like nothing matters. I hate him.

He's worth millions, and has fifteen women around him. It's like he's doing too much. Like he's being extra. He's done everything from lick the sides of their faces, to pour champagne on their breasts just to get attention. I really hope Aphrodite can trap this nigga now, because he deserves whatever he gets. But...with all that said, it's time for me to get to work.

I down the rest of the vodka in my cup, place it on the bar, and move toward the middle of the dance floor. First I sway my hips softly, like I'm waiting on my favorite beat to kick up, before I give it to them real nasty.

When I glance to my right, I see Killion is looking over here in my direction. So I start moving my hips wider, and larger until every nigga on the floor is gawking at me. When I glance over at Killion again, I see he's talking to a dude. Killion whispers in the man's ear, and they both look at me. I know immediately that I got him. He's probably about to send dude over here to get my attention.

When I see the five bottles of champagne that cost $500 a pop, I have an idea. Aphrodite gonna have a problem with me, because I'm not gonna get this nut for no measly one thousand dollars. For a nigga of this caliber he's worth at least two G's, and that's still playing myself short.

The dude is almost next to me, until I'm violently pulled backwards by someone. I'm just about to swing on whoever is putting their hands on me until I see Loop's face. He has tears in his eyes, and he looks frustrated with me. My heart drops immediately. What is he doing here?

"What's wrong, baby," I ask him. I'm trying to act innocent, but I know it's not working. "Are you okay?"

"Tell me it's not true."

"What?"

"Tell me you not up here about to fuck some nigga, for some nut. Tell me you wouldn't do that, when you know what it would do to me."

I'm not gonna lie, seeing him like this makes me feel powerful. He's so afraid in losing me that maybe he'll be willing to play hard with me again like I want. After all, he got me addicted to this shit, and it's unfair for me to wake up, only to see his life has changed and I'm still the same.

"Yes, I was gonna do it," I tell him, like I don't care. "What difference does it make, we two different people now, Loop. Remember? You clean, and got your life ahead of you, and all I want to do is escape my world, and get high. Maybe it's best if we just part ways."

"So you come down here, to fuck some nigga? Like we not even together no more?"

"Yes, I think it's over between us, Loop. You gotta do your thing, and I gotta do mine. I'm sorry." I turn around to walk toward Killion, when he snatches me again.

"Okay, baby, I'll do it."

I turn around and look at him. "You'll do what?" I want to hear him say the words.

"I'll do it with you one last time, but you gonna promise me that once we do this shit, that's it, Love. I don't want to be on this shit for the rest of my life. You don't understand, but since I've been clean, I have felt the best I have in my entire life. I can't stay down anymore, baby. I don't like the feeling of sleeping in no basement, waiting on you to give me my next pack. I want a chance at life."

"But at least we would be together."

"I'm serious," he yells. "One last time and that's it."

I hug him tightly and kiss him gently on the lips. He smells clean again, and something in me longs for the old smell. The dirty smell. The scent of hopelessness and needing me to be everything in his life. "Thank you, Loop," I say. "One last time and we done, I promise."

I kiss him again, and we walk toward the exit to leave the club. I see Killion staring at me from the corner of my eye, but I don't care. I'll leave my sister to all that nut swapping shit. All I want to do is be with my man, get high and forget my troubles.

When we make it outside I remember I don't understand something. "Loop, how you find out I was here? I didn't tell you."

"Nandi told me. Ya'll better be careful what you say around her. She's listening to everything."

by Candee

CHAPTER 20
J azzy

I have two bags of groceries in each hand, and I'm on the bus waiting for my stop. I had been dodging the Property Manager for the past few days, because he wants his money, or for us to leave the apartment, but I don't have anywhere else to go. To make things work, he had to believe we weren't home. So I demanded that Nandi stay out of the window, but only God knows for how much longer that would work. Its something about the world that she just had to be a part of, even though she acted like she didn't want to.

And then there was Love. At first I hoped she would come through for me, and get the shot from Killion we needed to pay the rent, but once again she let me down. To make matters worse, she did it without a reason or call. When I was in the bed, crying my eyes out, something came over me. Although I will do all I can to help Nandi, I have washed my hair officially with Love. If she wants to be on her own, smoke dope, and hang with Loop, I'm going to release her hand and let her go. A day passed since she left, and the truth is I had the best sleep of my life.

It's amazing, when you let go of the people you hold on to the most, I'm talking about Love and Cani, and you know you've given them your all, there's a strange peace that comes over you when you really let them go.

And that's where I am now. I'm good with not having Cani in my life, although I miss his companionship, and still love him.

When I see my stop coming up, I free my hands, ring the bell and wait for the bus to stop moving. I grab my bags, step off and I'm immediately slapped in the face by the brutal cold. The heavy gray smoke from the bus' exhaust pipe causes me to cough. The weather has been no joke lately, and it makes it hard to do what I have to, find somewhere safe for us to live.

As I walk up the street, towards my building, I can see the gaping hole covered in plastic, where Nandi's room use to be. I shake my head and sigh, because Killion's business practices are so messy. I fucking hate him! Although trapping Brad into a pregnancy for Kaitlin was business, if I could help Aphrodite get Killion, and get into his ass for millions, it would be my pleasure.

When I grab the door handle leading into my building, I can hear loud screaming. The sounds send chills down my spine, because it's so familiar. I drop my grocery bags where I am, next to the mailboxes, and rush toward the voice. The closer I get upstairs, I realize the inevitable, that the noise is coming from my apartment.

"What's going on," I ask when I see the backs of three men, and hear my sister crying for them to get out. I need somebody, anybody to tell me what's going on. Why is she so upset? Why are they here?

When one of the men turn around, I realize that he's Martin, the property manager. He has a clipboard in his hand and he approaches me with a serious attitude. "I told you, you had two weeks to pay the rent or get out. Didn't I? And you couldn't do it," he points at me with his pencil, and the eraser brushes against my nose. "Now I know you don't have nowhere to go, but I ain't married to you, and it ain't my problem. So you have to leave now."

"Martin, please, don't do this," I smile, "you know what I'm going through. If I had the money I would give it to you, you know that. All I need is a few more days, I got some things in the works."

"Again...not my problem."

I look at Nandi in my apartment, who is visibly shaken. Her face is wet with tears and she looks angry. "Nandi, go back inside. I want to talk—"

"You're not listening," Martin says interrupting me. "The inside of this apartment is not yours anymore. Now I want you and your sister out. Not tomorrow, but today."

I step back from him, place my hands on my hips and frown. "You got a wedding coming up don't you? You marrying Ms. Donna's daughter up the block. I just heard she got accepted into Harvard and everything, although I'm not sure how you roped her, because you gross me out. I heard you know how to eat a mean pussy, but since I never had the pleasure, I can't be sure. All you do to me is bend me over the desk and treat me like—"

"Why don't ya'll wait in my office," he tells his men. "I need to talk to Ms. Law in private."

As they walk downstairs, I tell Nandi to go back inside. She looks at me, and then at Martin and pulls the door shut. When the door is closed I say, "So now you understand—"

The moment I try to speak, my mouth is immediately slammed shut by a fist to my jaw. I fall to the ground, but he picks me up by my long hair, and hits me again in the lips and eye. I wiggle away from him just a little, and I'm face down on the ground, my nose is inches away from his black work boots. He picks my head up, and slams the clipboard over my head. I think he's trying to break it.

When he seems to be out of breath he looks down at me and says, "I want you and that crazy ass sister of yours out of this apartment in an hour. You better be glad I didn't charge you for the golf club she stole from me, even though I don't know how she got it. That's a sneaky little bitch." He reaches in his pocket, and I just know he's about to shoot me. "And here is one hundred dollars for the pussy shot you gave me in my office. It wasn't worth it. But, if you ever bring up what we did in my office again, I will kill you."

Nandi won't stop screaming. No matter how much I beg her, she won't stop. We're sitting in the U-Haul I rented, with the one hundred dollar bill Martin threw in my face. Everything we could fit inside of here we did, but I had to leave most of my furniture behind. I'm devastated and a dark cloud seems to hover over my head. Before I left, I saw Martin talking to Trudy upstairs, when I was taking my clothes out. He'll probably sell the rest of my stuff to her, and get back the money he gave me for the truck.

I thought about calling Kaitlin, to see if me and Nandi could stay with her for a little while, but I don't think it is safe. I never know what sets Nandi off, and I don't want my best friend hurt, or worst, killed if she gets Nandi wrong.

While Nandi is still wailing, I remove a water bottle from the grocery bag. It was the only grocery bag left, because my no good ass neighbors stole everything else while I was getting my ass whipped upstairs. At least they didn't get her new prescriptions, which I was able to get from the money I borrowed from Kaitlin yesterday. We are so in over our heads.

While Nandi is taking a break from crying, I hand her the water bottle and two Zoloft. She takes them without a fight or fuss. I guess she's tired of crying too. When she drinks the entire bottle of water she says, "I took pictures." She wipes the tears from her face. "I have them if you want them."

I lean back in the driver's seat, and turn up the heat to take the chill away. "Took pictures of what?"

"My face, when the ceiling came down. You wanna see them?"

I don't know what she's talking about, but I got time on my hands so I look at her. "Yeah, show me." She hands me a cell phone I didn't even know she had. "Where did you get this from?"

She frowns. "Mr. Johnson gives me what I want, if I give him some of my pills."

"You been giving that nigga your pills," I yell. "But why, Nandi? You need them."

"I don't need no medicine, Jazzy. It makes me sadder. And I give Mr. Johnson my pills for stuff that I want," she says flatly. "You want to see the pictures or not?"

I give her one more suspicious look and say, "Yeah, show me." She reaches over to the phone in my hand, and taps a few buttons. The screen brightens and a picture shows up with her bruised face. She's standing in the middle of the wreckage that was once her room and blood covers her forehead.

I look at her. "Nandi, I didn't know you were hurt when the walls came down. Why didn't you tell me? I mean, where is the cut?" I move her braids to the side, and notice the small gash. But what I also see is a few of her braids are missing, like they were snatched from her scalp. "Nandi, how did this happen?"

She yanks her head backwards and says, "Don't worry about all that. Worry about the picture."

I sit back in my seat and eye her cautiously. I would be lying if I didn't say she is scaring me. "What can I do with the picture? The man ain't fucking with us no more. I need to think of another place for us to go."

"You can stop being weak and go back upstairs, and tell that mothafucka that if he don't give us some more time, to pay rent, you gonna take that picture to the housing authority, and then you gonna file a lawsuit. And you tell him that we gonna get the money too, because I'm gonna go to the hospital and complain of headaches."

"How did you think of this idea, Nandi?"

She rolls her eyes. "I wish ya'll stop acting like I'm dumb. There's nothing more irritating then regular people always trying to make you think you crazy. I know some stuff, all you gotta do is ask." She turns back in her seat and looks out ahead of her. "Now go upstairs and put him straight, Jazzy. I did the hard work by giving you the picture, and I want to get back in my bed. I hate being out in the world too long, unless I got too. It makes me evil."

CHAPTER 21
Love

It was colder than ever and I tried to go home earlier tonight, but Jazzy wouldn't let me inside. I kept banging on the door, reminding her that my name was on the lease too, but she didn't care. And when I went to the rental office to complain, Martin told me to get the fuck out of his face. He seemed angry but, I'm not sure why.

I haven't seen Jazzy in two days, which is when I first left to meet Killion at the club. And since that time me and Loop been getting high, and it wasn't long before I realized that he does way more dope than me. Lately I had to earn some money, and cop from one of the dealers we didn't use together on the side, just to get my fix for the day. When I would come back to Loop, after being gone for about an hour to shoot my dope, he would frisk me all over my body, thinking I was hiding something.

It's crazy, at one point we had a lot of money. But we spent a thousand dollars that he got from God knows where, and when we went to cop again with the rest, the hustler's beat us and took everything else we have left.

So now here we are, with nothing to show for it. We were back in the laundry room, thinking about how to score, when I remembered Aphrodite needed that shot. So I called her, asked her if she still needed it, and she said yes. But she also said based on the ovulation kit she was using, she would either ovulate today or tomorrow, and she could no longer wait. So I decided to score this shot for her myself, and cut Jazzy out of the mix all together, since she wanted to be a bitch and not let me into the house. The thing is, I didn't tell Loop either, because no matter how broke we get, he has a problem with me fucking another dude for money. I guess he ain't been a dope head long enough, because I'm sure that will change soon.

I'm back in the club Killion likes, and I'm dancing to the music. It's not long before Killion sends his man over to me, and before long I'm back in VIP with his rich ass. Red soft couches sit against the wall, and gold bottles of champagne stuffed in mounds of white ice, sit in the middle of the table. About ten other girls are here too, and they give me nasty looks as I make my entrance. I don't let them stop my money though. I simply roll my eyes at each of them individually, and make my way toward the couches.

Once I'm there I take a seat on the space of the sofa, where nobody is sitting. I guess everyone else wants to show their dresses off, and the best way to do it is on your feet, because they are dancing all around me. But, I don't have time for that shit. I need this money, 'cause I'm feeling dope sick again.

"How you doing, sexy," Killion says to me, walking into my space. He tugs on the black NY Yankees cap on his head, and kisses me roughly on the lips, pressing his teeth into mine. "What you drinking?"

I wipe his spit juice off of my mouth and try not to frown. "Anything, I guess." He stuffs a champagne glass in my hand, grabs a gold bottle, and pours it into my cup. But when it's full, instead of stopping, he continues to tilt the bottle drenching my dress and shoes in the process. I'm about to go off on him, until he bends down, sticks his tongue in my mouth, and walks away. *Yuck!*

"What the fuck was that," I say to myself.

"Just relax," one of the girls says to me, handing me a towel, "at least he chose you." She's a pretty black and Chinese girl, with two fluffy ponytails sitting on top of her head. "He doesn't treat his showgirls the same, you'll be okay though."

What the fuck is a showgirl?

I wipe my dress, but it doesn't do any good. I'm done for as large wet stains sit all over my red dress. "Why does he have to act like that?" I throw the damp towel on the table.

"It doesn't matter, as long as he calls you, he'll look out for you, at least for the night anyway. After that he throws you away like he does everybody else. So you better get something out of it, if you can."

Two hours later I'm still sitting in the club, looking at Killion laugh it up with three other dudes, including one who is named Lewis, who keeps looking at me. He doesn't seem to like me. When my cell phone rings, I see its Aphrodite asking what's going on. I text her and tell her that I'm here, and the moment I got something for her, I'll let her know. I frown when I see her reply:

Don't like him too much Love. Remember this is a job, not pleasure.

by Candee

I don't even respond, because if I do decide to use this nigga for more than his nut, it won't be shit she can do about it but watch. I place my phone in my purse, and look up just as Killion is approaching me. Without words, he grabs my hand, and yanks me outside of the club. I don't know where we going or even why. I just know that he picked me, and that I'm even closer to getting paid.

We approach a car, and a driver opens the door for me, and then for him, and we slip into the back of a black Maybach. Once the doors are closed Killion pulls me closer to him, and I can smell the musty scent of his underarms. I guess cause he's been moving around all day, but after dealing with Loop's natural odor for years, it doesn't bother me that much.

"Take me to my place, Alto."

The driver in the front seat looks back at him, and then at me. "Are you sure? You never take anybody home."

"Don't ever make me repeat myself again," he tells him, "now drive."

Wow, he's taking me to his house? Some place he doesn't take other girls? I guess I'm not just for show after all. I'm smiling widely until I receive a text from Aphrodite again. I ease away from Killion, because I don't want him to see her name or message. It was dumb of me to program her number with the right name, but hindsight is twenty-twenty I guess.

Don't fuc me over. If I find out you are crossing me, I'll let Jazzy know about our little deal to cut her out. He belongs 2 me.

After reading her message I throw the phone back in my purse. Fuck that bitch, it ain't like Jazz is talking to me anyway, she already cut me off.

"You okay," Killion asks me.

I look over at him. He is smiling and doesn't seem as arrogant as he did about an hour ago. When he's outside of the club he's kind of cool, and I like him like this. "I'm fine. My friend was just getting on my nerves that's all."

"Well don't let anybody spoil your night who is not here to share it with you."

I grin. "You're right."

"I know I am," he smiles. "I always am. Now lets go have a good time."

The moment I walk into Killion's house, I am in awe. Now that I'm in his home, for some reason I thought about Loop, when my heels clicked across his cream marble floors, and I am led into a large spacious living room, with a wooden fireplace which was already glowing, I wonder if me and Loop would've had the same lifestyle, had he never fell down the steps that day, and lost his career.

"Come back here," Killion says grabbing my hand.

I follow him past the cherry wood walls, and into a bedroom three times the size of our apartment. A small ball of hate rolls through my body, because I think about how we lived in his fucked up ass building, while he lives like a star.

"Sit down over there," he says pointing to a burgundy leather couch at the end of his bed.

I take a seat and he grabs a remote control the size of an iPad. He aims it at a mirror and it turns into a TV before my eyes. I'm blown away at how crystal clear the picture is, and I'm transported to a movie theater. I've never seen anything so beautiful in all of my life. I feel like I'm home, until I get another text from crazy girl.

What's going on? U get it or what?

I don't respond, but I keep my phone in my hand, and a second later she hits me up again.

U fucked up by not answering my texts. Now I'll show you what kind of bitch I can really be.

Afraid of what she might do, I text her back quickly.

Me: I said I'm gonna get you the shot. Relax!
Her: Too late.

There's nothing I can do about it, so I throw my phone into my purse. I'm watching a reality TV show, when Killion comes back in front of me with a gold bottle of champagne and a crystal flute. He hands the glass to me, and pours. "That's it," I say trying to prevent him from spilling it over my clothes again.

He laughs. "I'm not gonna wet you up again," he stops right before the suds from the champagne pours over my fingers. I lick it off. "Don't do that."

"Do what?"

"Lick your fingers." He tilts the bottle to his lips, sticks his tongue into the spout and drinks.

I giggle. "Stop being bad."

"You haven't seen bad yet," he says placing the bottle down on the table.

"Why did you pick me," I ask.

He laughs, and runs his hand down my cheek. Like I'm some stupid little girl. "Does it make a difference?"

"I want to know."

"You seem a little rough around the edges, and I like girls that are rough around the edges. Question, you fuck with that nigga I saw you with at the club don't you?"

My heart drops. Why is he asking about him? "Not really."

"Good, because he doesn't deserve you. I'm gonna steal you away from him."

What does he want with me? And will he tell Loop I was here? I'm worried and turned on at the same time. Killion zips down his pants, and removes his dick, without an invitation. He isn't circumcised and I tried to hide my disgust. The meat flaps over his pee hole, and makes it difficult to think of it as a dick. It resembles some sort of strange creature.

I place the champagne glass against my lips, so he doesn't want a dick suck. "You got condoms right?"

"I don't want to fuck you," he frowns. "I want to see what them jaws feel like." He removes the glass from my hand, and places the tip of his dick against my bottom lip. The loose salty meat brushes against my teeth and I want to run. My mind is all over the place until I realize something. Even if I try to get the shot for Aphrodite, I don't have anything to put it in. I'm not prepared for this type of shit. So I turn my head and ask, "You got a paper cup?"

He frowns down at me. "A paper cup for what?"

"I wanted to get some water. All this drinking has my mouth dry."

"Get some water later. Drink champagne."

He tries to stick his dick into my mouth again but this time his phone rings. "Fuck," he yells walking toward his end table, pulling his pants up once he's there. "Niggas always hitting me at the wrong damn time." He picks up his cell phone, looks at the message and then slowly turns his head towards me.

The last time a person looked at me in that way, Cyrus had threatened our lives when he opened the freezer and saw us inside, minutes after he killed my sister. I got the impression that if the cops weren't there, that he would've murdered us in cold blood too, and I get the same impression from Killion now. I know immediately that Aphrodite told him what I was here to do, and that my life was in danger.

He throws his cell phone on his bed and hustles over towards me. I stand up and say, "I'm kinda tired, Killion." I place the champagne down. "You mind taking me home? I didn't realize it was so late and I have to take my sister to a doctor's appointment in the morning."

"Who are you," he asks standing in my face. It's like I walked into his home without his knowledge.

"I told you in the car, my name is Evangeline."

He glares. "You told me your name was Erica."

I start shaking. I'm so scared that I forgot everything I told him. I didn't think what would happen if he caught me in my lie. "Evangeline is my middle name. My first name is Erica."

I don't know how he got to it, but he grabs the champagne flute I was drinking from, and comes down over my face. I can feel my right cheek open up, and my thick blood ooze down my neck. The wound stings terribly, and I place my hands over it, trying to stop the blood from flowing.

"Who are you?" he repeats.

"I'm...I...I'm..."

Before I can lie again, he balls his fist up and punches me square in the nose. I'm dizzy and I see white stars. I place my fingers over my face, because I can feel that he's broken the bones. Blood fills up in my mouth and I tumble to the floor. With his boots, he kicks me over and over in the gut, and strips me of my clothes and shoes. I'm thinking he's about to rape me, but instead he grabs me by the hair, and throws me out of the door, into the cold.

CHAPTER 22
J azzy

"Girl, it's cool, I'm on my way to his tennis shoe shop right now," I tell Aphrodite on the phone, as I maneuver her silver BMW down the street as if it were mine. This car feels so much like me, and I can't wait to finally get my life on track so I can cop something like this. "Thanks for letting me use your car too. I know you didn't have to do this."

"That ain't about nothing, Jazzy. I'm just sorry I let your sister lie to me and tell me she was still working for you. You should've heard her, talking about if you want to get at Killion, you gotta go through me. She was wilding out on you, Jazzy. You gotta watch your sister."

Aphrodite's getting on my nerves. I heard this story in five different ways since she called me this morning and told me she still needed my help. "Yeah, that's pretty fucked up."

"I'm not gonna lie," she continues. "The way she was acting, she made me think she didn't fuck with you like that. Your own flesh and blood! Talking about how you put her out of the house, and shit. It was bad, Jazz. Real bad. And then she had the nerve not to get served by Killion. Niggas around town talking about how he put her out on her ass with no clothes. I feel bad about that part, because I know she is your family, but you can't do people wrong and think things are cool." This bitch acting like she not trying to trap a nigga into a pregnancy. "Just so you know, I ain't have nothing to do with Killion getting the call about Love trying to set him up."

"Aphrodite, I got two things for you so let me give them to you quickly. Number one, only my friends call me Jazz. Number two, I don't talk to people I don't know that well about my sister, that's family business and it will remain as so. Now Love got her shit with her, and we gonna deal with that when it's time, but that's between me and her. Got it?"

"Oh…I didn't mean it like that."

"I know, and it ain't your fault that you were talking recklessly, you just didn't know me like that. But, now you do. So don't ever come at me about my family like that again. Cool?"

"Cool." She sighs.

I hate to go on old girl like this, but she jumped out of the window by coming at me about Love. Don't get me wrong; Love is done for when it comes to me. And although I love her, I will never allow her in my house again, but that's still our business, and not hers.

We agree on one thing, Love really played herself by trying to do the job alone. I still couldn't believe it when the property manager knocked on the door this morning, to tell me what happened to Love. The smile on his face was wide, as he brought me the bad news. He loved the look on my face when I heard what happened to my sister.

"Just so you know Killion fucked your sister up for trying to rob him last night," he laughed. "That's what happens when bitches try to get over."

"Fuck you," I yelled at him, slamming the door into his face.

Martin was already mad about that picture Nandi gave me to show him, of her bruised face from when the ceiling came crashing down around her. It was because of the picture that he gave me one last week, to come up with the money for the apartment. That's why doing this for Aphrodite is my last opportunity. It's my only chance.

"Aphrodite, I'm at Killion's tennis shoe spot right now, I'll call you when I have more information."

"Please call me back, Jazzy. I really need that—"

"You been pressing me a lot lately," I say cutting her off. "I said I will hit you back the moment I get some information. You can't make me get it no quicker by coming at me all hard and shit."

"I don't mean to be coming at you disrespectfully, but I'm ovulating. So I only got between today and to-morrow to inseminate. I would try to do it myself, but Killion isn't taking any of my calls. You are my only hope."

"So relax and let me do my job, and I'll call you when I can...bye."

When I hang up on her, I park a few stores down from Killion's shop. I can see the Neon sign that reads *The Right Fit.* I also see his black Maybach at the curb with somebody standing next to it, with his hands clasped in front of his body. He must be the driver.

Upscale KITTENS

After about an hour, I see Killion bop outside, wearing a brown fur coat, and his butter colored Timberland boots. The driver opens his car door for him. I bend down in the driver seat, because I don't know if Killion will recognize Aphrodite's car or not. When Killion slides into the car, I follow them about three miles out, to some tall brick building. I know he owns this too, because he owns most of the slummy property in DC. And the building is leaning over so much it looks like it will smash against the streets.

The driver parks, but this time he stays inside. He doesn't even open the door for his boss. Seconds later Killion hops out, and enters an apartment on the ground level with a set of keys. The moment I think he's in there handling business, I see Faggy Bernard take some keys out of his pocket, and open the door to the same apartment Killion entered. My jaw drops because Bernard has been known around DC to fuck with gay drug dealers, and now I'm getting proof that Killion is gay too. I'm also immediately sad, because Bernard and I have a history. A sad history.

After fifteen minutes, and five text messages from Aphrodite, Killion finally comes out, gets into his car and pulls off. Bernard is in the apartment for fifteen more minutes before he exits too.

I'm nervous about what I'm going to do, because I don't know if it will work or not, but I jump out there anyway. I beep the horn three times and wave Bernard over towards me. At first he reaches into the gold purse that dangles from his shoulder, I guess to grab his knife if needed.

161

I lean my head out of the driver's window and yell, "Bernard, it's me, Jazzy!"

He bends down a little and focuses on the car. "Is that you, my J. Law," he smiles walking over to the car. "Oh my, stars it's been so long!" He's so excited to see me and I can't help but grin. Bernard and I have good and bad history, so it's good to know he chooses to focus on the great parts, instead of the awful.

"I know, I been trying to survive. What about you?"

"Shit, I ain't doing nothing but trying to keep my head above water, you know how I do out here in these streets." He looks at the car. "It looks like you made a life for yourself, nice wheels. I'm so proud of you."

"It ain't mine."

"Story of my life when it comes to men, chile," he laughs. "Unfortunately I only get the broke ass niggas these days. I swear they gonna be the death of the ole girl, honey. If I let them anyway."

My heart is beating fast now, because I don't know if he'll accept the proposition I have for him. Instead of beating around the bush, I decide to get right down to it.

"I got a job for you that will earn you some money, if you up for it."

"At this point in my life, Jazzy, I'm up for anything, baby."

Bernard and me are sitting at the table in my apartment, drinking wine. I forgot how much fun he is to be around, because I hadn't seen him since the first apartment that was condemned. Back in the day when I needed somebody to sit with Nandi while I was at work, he would do it with no questions asked. He was an all around good friend, and just plain lovable.

At one point he had to leave his apartment in Northwest DC, because he fucked this married guy named Marcus, who was trying to kill him because his wife found out. She threatened to divorce him, unless he put Bernard deep into the ground, and she meant it. When Bernard didn't have anywhere to go, I let him stay with me, and things were good, until I got serious with Cani.

Instead of giving Bernard a chance, Cani took one look at him, formed his opinions and made me put him out on the streets. If there was one thing Cani couldn't deal with, it was men who dealt with other men. At one point I thought he was secretly gay, because he hated them so much. But after some time, it became clear that his hate was pure. He didn't like faggies, and he didn't want them anywhere near him.

Putting Bernard out was the hardest thing I ever had to do, because Bernard wasn't just something to do for fun. He was family and I loved him dearly, I still love him now. But just like the real bitch that he is, he never held a grudge against me. Besides, once he left my apartment, some old white real estate mogul, who put him up in the new high rises in Federal Hill, caught him and laced him up good. Gave him a life to die for.

Mr. Posh did everything for Bernard, but when some Southeast niggas robbed his house, he put Bernard out thinking he had something to do with it. Bernard swore his innocence to everyone who listened and I believed him, because he wasn't the type of dude to set up some-one who was good to him. He did his dirt, but he had a code too.

After some time word got around that it was Marcus who robbed Mr. Posh, but it couldn't be proven because days later Marcus was shot in the eye while sitting in his car, waiting on his wife to come out of the beauty salon. When people asked Bernard if he was involved, he would say, *girls never tell their secrets.*

"So tell me how you hooked up with Killion," I ask pouring him another glass of wine. "I could never pic-ture you with somebody like him."

"Girl, it's a long story. After Mr. Posh was robbed, I was on the streets and times were dreadful. I didn't have a place to go, and I thought about killing myself. It was that bad, Jazzy."

It hurts my heart to hear him talk like that. Bernard was always so strong.

"Anyway, Killion got in contact with me, and put me in that apartment you saw me coming out of. It ain't the best place to live in the world, honey, but it's free and it's mine." He sips his wine. "Girl, but the nigga's a slumlord. If the walls ain't leaking, the toilets are over-flowing. I tell Killion all the time that he needs to fix that building but he don't care."

"That's sad," I say shaking my head, remembering what happened to Nandi.

"It is, and it wasn't until the other day that I found out he was selling his properties off to this real estate developer, for an exuberant amount of money. Jazzy, they gonna tear down all of his buildings, and build up new ones, including this one. When the deal is done, chile Killion will be a billionaire."

My jaw drops. "How do you know?"

"I'm fucking the nigga, girl," he laughs. "If I don't know shit else I know his business and where his paper coming in at."

"So if he looks out for you, why do you want to do this job?"

He sighs. "True, he does look out for me, but Killion is also mean. *Real mean.*" He shakes his head. "I've dealt with Night Faggies all my life, you know the ones, who only want to love you when the moon goes down, and the sky is dark. But he is by far the meanest trade of them all. He doesn't give me no money, and he's a liar."

"Why you say that?"

"Well when I first got with him, he ran this game with his driver on me. I was working for a donut shop at the time, and he walks in, takes one look at me and smiles. While I was packing his order, he asked me to meet him later that night when I got off of work. When I got off, I did just that. The moment I got outside I saw the prettiest car I ever seen in my life. Now, Mr. Posh was rich, but he didn't believe in beautiful cars, so this was a first for me.

Anyway, honey, the driver opens the door for me, and we both get inside. Then Killion tells him to take me to his house. Instead of pulling off the driver gonna say, *but you never take anybody there.* So Killion tells him to do it anyway, girl. That's how he got me to thinking I was special and all, because he took me to his house that no one else went to. Turns out that was his mother's crib. Shit, that was the first time I saw a mirror turn into a TV," he laughs.

"Where his mother stay if she ain't at the house?"

"She spends most of her time in her house in Southwest, so he uses the other house as his bachelor's pad. To this day I don't know where he lives for real. But all of his faggies been to his mother's, even his new faggy Loop."

"W-what…what you mean?" My jaw hangs although I try to pick it up.

Bernard gently pushes my mouth closed. "Girl, you know him?"

"Yeah, Love use to deal with him," I say. I didn't want him to know they were still dealing now. I guess I'm too embarrassed.

"Girl, yes, Killion be banging Loop's back out! Tell your sister to beware. He fucked that little boy every which way but loose! Anyway, Loop use to fuck with that dope, but Killion cleaned him up, and been giving him money and everything. Although I heard he started fucking with that shit again. It's so sad what heroin can do to you."

"This shit is crazy."

"Girl, it sure is. It was Loop who called Killion and told him that some dope head was trying to rob him last night. I heard he beat the hell out of the girl and put her out on the street. He told me when we were together just now."

My feelings are hurt when I think about Love. And for a moment I consider going out to look for her. But, I know she will never leave Loop, and I can't deal with that pain or her hurting my feelings anymore. I really have to let her go. I don't even tell Bernard that Love was with him now, and that she was the one who got beat.

But Loop fucking Killion though? I can't believe Loop would fall so low.

"Are you okay, baby," Bernard says rubbing my hand.

I look up at him, wipe away the tears I didn't know crept on my face before now and say, "I'm fine."

"Enough of talking about dead beat niggas," he says wiping at the air, "tell me about this job you got going for me. Whatever plans you got for Killion I'm with."

"Before we do that, if Killion is gay, how come he has women around him all of the time," I ask.

"Oh, chile, he believes in stunts and shows," he says. "He calls them his showgirls, the ones who drape his arm out in public. He'll even let a female suck his dick, and shit like that, but he gotta be real mean to them when he does it too. That's the only way he can get off with a woman. He likes to have at least a few females out in the world who can vouch for him being hetero-sexual. It's all for show. But when he's with me, he always gives me the truth."

"That's wild."

"No, that's Killion," he giggles. "Poor thing got all that money in the world, but he's still afraid to be who he is." He shrugs. "Anyway, give me the plan. I'm ready to get paid."

I tell him how I need him to collect Killion's sperm in some plastic, and that I need it tonight. I tell him I'll pay him $500.00, and his face brightens. He said he was having hard times so the money would come just in time, and I know just how he felt. I planned to use the other $500 I was getting to pay my bills too, until I came up with another plan for the next month's rent.

A part of me thought about the fact that if Bernard wants to, he could go somewhere, bust off into the plastic himself, and pass it off as Killion's nut. There would be no way I would know the difference, until Aphrodite's baby is born.

"You know I wouldn't do that right," he says, waking me out of my thoughts.

"Do what?"

"Pass off something else like it's Killion's," he says to me. "I need this money, but you looked out for me when I really needed somebody. I care about you, Jazzy. And I remember how even when Cani gave you the ultimatum, to get rid of me or lose him, you begged him from 5 pm the day before, until 9 am the next morning to change his mine. Your eyes were red, and I could feel your love for me," he pauses. "I still feel it now. Killion deserves this shit and I want to do this for you, and me too. Besides, the nigga's rich, he got enough money, and it's time to share. What he gonna do with all of it anyway."

I hug him. "Thank you so much, Bernard."

"This ain't about nothing," he sighs. "Well, let me convince this nigga to come back over my place tonight, so we can get this shit over with. It shouldn't be hard, he's in love with the old girl. It's money time!"

Bernard was on his shit, three hours later he was back in my apartment, with the shot in the plastic I gave him. I called Aphrodite over, and she inseminated herself in my bathroom with my turkey baster. I threw it in trash when she was done. I won't be using that shit again.

Instead of leaving, the three of us drank some wine, which she claimed would be her last time, since she hoped to be pregnant. I'm not gonna lie, the more time I spent around her, the more I started to think she was a lunatic. It was the way her eyes rolled around, and how she never seemed to care about what you thought, even though she asked you constant questions.

And then there was the thing with Bernard being gay. When I told her Killion was fucking niggas, and that Bernard had to get the shot for her instead of me, she still didn't seem to mind. I mean I would be fucked up if I had to go this far to get pregnant, but she doesn't care. Bernard told her how he jerked him off, got the shot when he wasn't looking, and how he fucked him again afterwards, so he wouldn't suspect anything. To be honest that was the only time I saw an expression from her. When she learned after cumming once, they were intimate again.

"So I'm about to go, girl," Aphrodite says, "Here's the money I owe you."

She reaches into her purse and hands me five one hundred dollar bills, and a blue piece of paper. My heart drops when I see the paper. I didn't agree to a check, and she knows it. But, I don't want to do this in front of

Bernard. He got what we needed, so I need him to go, to speak to her in private.

"Bernard, here's your money, honey," I tell him handing him the cash. "I'll call you later."

Instead of leaving right away, he looks at his money and the blue piece of paper. "You okay, girly? Cause I can stay here a little longer until things clear up." He eyes Aphrodite suspiciously. "Just say the word." That meant he could cut her, and help me dump her body if I asked.

"No, I'm good," I say touching his hand. "Go get some rest, you've had a rough day." He looks at me once more, hugs me and then leaves.

When the door closes she jumps right to it. "Before you get mad about the check let me explain."

"This is not what we agreed on! I need this money! You know what I'm going through, I told you. These mothafuckas trying to throw us out on the streets."

"I know but please understand that my checks don't bounce. I had to give you five hundred cash and the rest on a check, because I got this after the bank closed. It's midnight, Jazzy. $500 a night is my ATM limit."

"Aphrodite, you got what you asked for, but I didn't. This shit ain't fair."

"And like I said, the check is good. Relax, Jazz."

"Bitch, I told you to call me Jazzy."

"You know what," she says grabbing her coat and purse angrily, "I'm out of here. When you go to the bank in the morning, and that check clears, I'll be waiting on my apology."

I'm about to snatch her hair out of her scalp, until Nandi walks into the living room. My blood runs cold; as I see a knife dangle from her hand.

"Just leave, Aphrodite."

She takes one look at Nandi, laughs and walks out.

When she leaves I sit on the couch and pray that this check actually cashes, if it doesn't I'm screwed.

CHAPTER 23
A phrodite

The sunlight crept through the windows in Killion's mother's house, as Aphrodite lay in his bed looking at him sleep. Aphrodite wasn't totally honest with Jazzy and Love about her relationship with him. Not only had she never been with Killion sexually, outside of sucking his dick, she met him through her brother Roscoe, who Killion was fucking on the side. They had never been in a relationship.

From the moment she laid eyes on him, she had become obsessed with Killion. At first he would humor her, but when it was obvious that she wanted more than he was willing to provide, he cut her brother off, and her too. Although her brother got the picture, she kept calling him, and he grew frustrated. At one point he even threatened her life, but still Aphrodite didn't get the message. She would show up at the clubs he frequented, and did all she could to get his attention. When he beat her so badly a few months back, she stopped her attempts, and decided to try a different approach. That's when she found out about Jazzy through their mutual friend Kaitlin.

The only way Aphrodite was able to get into his house last night was because although Killion didn't know it, she was a regular over his mother's house. She pretended to be the nice girl who lived up the block from his mother, who would help her with her groceries, and keep her company when Killion couldn't. Before long Aphrodite won Mrs. Holmes over, and she was able to clip her keys off of Mrs. Holmes ring, to her big house that Killion loved.

Killion stirred a little in the bed, before yawning and opening his eyes. He rolled over, trying to get some more sleep when his body told him he was still tired. But the moment he saw her smiling at him on the other side of the bed, he hopped up in anger.

"What the fuck you doing in my house," he yelled. "How did you get in here?"

She sat up in the bed and tried to smile. "What are you talking about, baby? You invited me, remember," she grinned.

"What the fuck you doing in my house, bitch," he repeated, this time more angrily. "I ain't never been that drunk before. To deal with no bitch."

"I told you, you invited me over," when she saw how irritated he was, she tapped the 911 button on her phone under the sheets. "You said you wanted to see me and that you were sorry for how we ended things. Think about it, Killion, how else would I get in? We made love and everything, don't you remember?"

"Why the fuck you lying to me? I never fucked with you, and I never liked you." He pulled a gun out of his drawer, cocked it, and aimed in her direction. "Now I'm gonna ask you again, how the fuck did you get into my house?"

by Candee

She could hear the operator saying 911 what is your emergency, from under the sheets. Killion was so angry that he didn't hear the voice.

Realizing her life was in danger she did what she always did, lie. "Bernard took the key off of your ring and gave it to me. I met him one night and I'm at 9834 Dale Lane, in Clinton Maryland." She wanted the 911 operators to know where she was, before he took her life.

"What the fuck are you talking about," he asked.

She raised the phone in her hand, and he frowned.

CHAPTER 24
Jazzy

When I hear a loud sound at the front door, like someone kicked it in, I jump up, grab my robe, and move toward Nandi's room. But before I can get there, in my living room I see Martin standing with five men.

"What the fuck you doing in my house," I ask tying my robe closed. "You can't come in here like this."

"You got my money," he asks. "If you don't, there ain't shit you can say to me no more, and this ain't our apartment. I'm done with the games."

I rush toward the kitchen table and grab the check, Aphrodite gave me last night. "Here it is right here. I just gotta cash it and I can give you your rent. I promise you, you'll have your cash today."

"That's not working for me this time," he looks at the men. "Take everything in here, and put it out on the streets. That includes their bodies."

When one of the men move toward Nandi's room, I jump on his back and ride him like a coat. I'm clawing at his eyes, and neck, because I don't want them to touch her. While I'm on him, one of the other men rushes into her room anyway, and grabs her forcefully by the arms. He's so rough with handling her arms, that I fear he's about to snatch her shoulder out of the socket.

Nandi is kicking and waving her fists wildly, and before I know it, she has grabbed a hold of Martin, and is biting him on the shoulders, like a vampire. Martin, with one wave of his hand, flings her off, and her head knocks against the wall.

I don't know how I get away from the guy who is holding me, but when I do escape, I'm in Martin's face, punching and kicking him everywhere my fists will land. Before long it becomes clear that they are men, and we are women, because we are thrown in the hallway, half naked and with our clothes being thrown in our faces.

When I try to get back inside, to at least grab my purse, I am smacked in the eye with the strap to my pocketbook, because Martin threw it at me. They are not even near being nice, and I'm trapped in emotion, trying to figure out how and why Martin would go so far to get rid of us, but I know it won't matter even if I got an answer.

Nandi and I grab a few items from the hallway floor, slide it over our bodies, and pick up what's most important to us.

People are coming out of their apartments until he says, "Unless you want the same thing to happen to you, mind your fucking business and go back inside. Now!" They close their doors one by one.

Martin comes out of the hallway and says, "I told Killion about the tenants in 5B, who are blackmailing him by staying in his apartment without paying. He wasn't happy about it. Now for your sake, I didn't give him your names, so consider that a gift."

I know the only reason he didn't tell Killion who we were was because he fucked me for rent, and he probably doesn't want him to know.

"Because if he knew who you were, he wouldn't hesitate to have you dealt with. Now despite the unprofessional way you choose to handle the matter, he's willing to be neighborly by giving you the U-Haul that's out front to get your things off of his property. And do yourself a favor, don't ever come back here again, for anything."

I'm sitting in the driver's seat of the U-Haul truck, and Nandi is sitting in the passenger seat. I can't even cry anymore. The check Aphrodite gave me bounced, and she wouldn't answer her phone when I called to question her about it. I was depending on that money to get us a better place, and now it was all in vain.

"I'm sorry I failed you, Nandi," I say, looking over at her. "I'm so sorry I let you down."

"Stop feeling bad for yourself, Jazzy," she sighs, "I'm tired of that shit.

I look over at her. "Did you take your meds today?"

"No," she says dryly, "Unfortunately I was snatched out of my bedroom, before I had a chance to do anything. Remember? Stop being so stupid, Jazzy. It makes me angry."

Nandi is different now. I can always tell when she isn't medicated because she becomes angry. But since she's like this, I decide to ask the serious questions I wanted to know, but was too afraid to. "You killed her didn't you—Starr."

She looks over at me. "Yes."

"Why?"

"She was fucking Cani," she says. "In your house. It's because of her he ran away and left us alone. In my opinion she had to go, so I took care of it."

My temples throb and I feel hot all over. "How...how do you know they were sleeping together?"

"I've known for a while, Love did too." My heart breaks even more. "So I went over there and did something about it."

"When?"

"It happened after you left to go to the hospital, when Love took that hot shot, and almost died. I knocked on the door, asked her if I could use her phone, because I was alone and scared, and she let me inside."

"I'm confused," I say.

"Don't be. I went for her kitchen, where she said the phone was, and grabbed a knife from the drawer. Then I put it behind my back, picked up the phone, and pretended to call someone. She walked toward me, and the minute she did, I stabbed her in the stomach repeatedly." She starts laughing. "The stupid slut grabbed my braids, and snatched a few of them out by the roots, trying to fight me. That's why I've been wearing my braids to the side, to hide the ones that are gone." She shakes her head. "I saw them in her dead hand, took them, and wiped my fingerprints off of the phone, since that was the only place I touched. The thing was, I thought she was dead when I left, but she wasn't and made it to her front door. How she got her toe caught in the door is beyond me, but about that time I was long gone."

"Nandi, no," I say.

"Jazzy, please. That bitch was a mess. I almost killed her before, but Love came home and caught me that time. I wasn't going to ruin my chance again."

My eyes widen. "What do you mean?"

"You were at work, and Cani thought I was sleep in my room. Starr came over from next door, to borrow some sugar like she did every time you were at work and he was home watching me. Normally he wouldn't let her in, and would slam the door in her face, but this time was different. When she was inside she kept begging him to give her a chance to make him feel good, and I was so mad, Jazzy. I cracked my room door, and could see her grabbing at him. He did everything he could to make her stop, but she wouldn't go away. She acted like she couldn't leave him alone. Or live without him." She sighs. "And it made me so mad. It still makes me mad now."

"This is so crazy," I say under my breath.

"Anyway, he ran toward the bathroom, and she followed him in there. He said she wasn't trying to do nothing but fuck up his relationship and life with you. When I peeked my head out, and saw they both were in the bathroom, I went into the kitchen and grabbed a knife. Then I went into the living room closet and hid, because I was going to stab Starr on her way out. But Love came home, and when she was about to put her jacket up, she saw me inside with the knife.

"She was about to try to pull me out of the closet, until she heard the voices in the bathroom too. She got inside with me, and through the crack of the door, we both saw Cani and Starr coming out of the bathroom. He was getting weaker, and before I knew it, he was bending her over on the sofa, having sex with her." Nandi cries. "I didn't blame Cani though, he fought back as best as he could. But Starr got naked right there in the living room, and was just begging him to fuck her."

"But you told me he slapped her for trying to come at him."

"I know, I lied. He deserved a good lie. He tried to get her to stop, Jazzy don't you see?" She shakes her head. "After Starr went home, and Love pushed me into the bedroom, she tried to give me some of my pills to make me forget. But I told her Cani gave me a few already, so she could just leave me alone. I faked tired, and sleepy and she left it alone. Sometimes the pills make me dizzy, and I don't like them. She told me not to tell you about what I saw, because she would get at Cani in another way, but I never knew how."

I'm looking over at her, scared and confused. This isn't the little girl I grew up with, before Angela died. "Was there anyone else?" I swallowed. "That you killed?"

"Do you really want to know?"

I nod yes.

"Well, there was almost Loop. I heard you arguing at him when he was yelling and telling everybody who would listen that he had gotten a NBA deal. So on Valentines Day, when he knocked on the door with roses, and asked if Love was home, I invited him inside."

"Where was Tabitha? She was supposed to be watching you that day."

"Jazzy, don't be stupid," she giggles. "You and me both know that girl did anything but work. Anyway, once Loop came inside the apartment, I convinced him to let me make things real romantic for Love, since they had been arguing. It was my idea to place the rose petals on the steps, but what he didn't know was that I also poured some baby oil on them too. I don't know how he got down them first, without slipping and falling. I guess the extra weight he had with Love, when he was walking back up the stairs was what was needed. So when he went tumbling down the stairs, I assumed he was dead. I never knew he was going to carry Love up-stairs, but I'm glad she was okay. That death plan was not meant for her."

"Is there anyone else?" I say, as tears crawl down my face.

"Well, kinda, you see Mr. Johnson told me that Loop was messing with Love again, and that nobody knew. So I convinced him to talk to Brandon, and give him a bottle of my Percocet pills, if he would sell Love a hot shot that I thought she would give to Loop. The only thing is, Love used it herself, and almost died. I felt bad for that one. It had Loop's name all over it."

"Nandi, is there anyone else," I ask, as my teeth knock against each other.

"Mommy. I killed her too. Gave her something to put her to sleep for good. I'd seen her do it to her best friend Victoria, who came over the house and stole her checkbook that one time. Poor Victoria died the same day, when mama put rat poisoning in her baggy. I put rat poisoning in mama's baggy too and took care of her."

I'm crying so hard I can barely see her. "Nandi...why? Why are you this way?"

"Because mama was a liar," she frowns. "She would promise to take care of us, and do things for us, but she never came through. The last time she promised to take us to the circus, and she didn't show up, and I was sad, because I wanted to see the lions from that TV commercial, made me hurt her even more."

"Nandi, I thought you didn't like to come out of your room."

"I don't like to come out when people are up, or watching me. But when it's just me, and nobody is around, I like it that way."

"I have to get you some help. You need to see somebody that can take care of you, and show you how to deal with your instincts. Killing people is not normal. Don't you see?"

"I don't need any help," she frowns.

"Nandi, you need help, and I'm gonna get you some."

"If you tell anybody about anything I did, I'll tell them about what you did to Mrs. Bickers. And how you helped me cover up the crime. So stop saying things you don't mean, Jazzy. I'm not going anywhere, and I don't need no help. What you need to be doing is thinking on how we can get some money, because I don't think we can live in this truck forever. Do you?"

My sister is insane. The type of insane that needs an in-house facility. So I leave the truck, to clear my mind. Everything Nandi has told me tonight, weighs on my head. Nandi is sicker than I ever imagined. Yes I knew what she did at Blooming Flowers Group Home, but at the time I felt it was warranted. I really did. That woman was abusive, and may have killed one of us if she didn't hit her over the head with the statue.

But mama, and Starr? And Loop? It was all so crazy. As I walk a block up the dark street, it's starts to rain heavily. I look back at the U-Haul, and it's partially hidden in the heavy downpour falling from the sky. My hair flattens under the pressure of the storm, and I cry to myself. A deep cry, the kind that could heal me if I had a solution for what was happening in my life. But I don't have a plan. We are broke, my sister is nutty, and my other sister is out there in the world somewhere without me using drugs. I don't know what to do anymore and I failed Angela by not keeping my sisters together and safe.

I continue to walk in the rain, until I see another woman holding a red umbrella. She's wearing a huge smile on her face, and she seems as if nothing else in the world matters. I'm jealous immediately. Oddly enough, she looks familiar.

When she gets close enough to me I say, "Mam, I don't mean to bother you, but I'm in a terrible bind. I wouldn't ask you this if I had any other recourse, but do you have any money you could give me? Any at all? I'll take anything."

"Are you okay, young lady," she asks, with caring eyes from up under her umbrella. "You're going to catch a cold." She steps closer to me, and allows me to share her umbrella.

"I'm not doing well at all," I say wiping the water out of my eyes, "and I don't want to burden you with the details. But, if you could spare any money, any money at all, it would be greatly appreciated."

She looks me into my eyes, digs into her pocket, and hands me some cash. Although the rain dampens the bills, I can still see the denominations. It's a fifty and one hundred-dollar bill.

"Mam, I...I..."

"Don't worry about it," she smiles, "I remember you from Smalls. You were helping the cashier bag my groceries. When that dirty old man came onto you, I think he was your boss or something. I remember being so proud of you for standing up to him for what you believed. Its not easy finding jobs out here, so that was very brave." She looks out ahead of her. "Well, I hope that can help you out a little. Its all I can spare. Good luck."

The moment she walks off, rain pours over my head again. I cry deep and hard for the woman who didn't know me, but still offered me kindness. Somebody helped me who didn't know me, and I am so grateful. I think it is Angela, who is assisting me from up above. I also know in this moment that when I get back on my feet, I will never fall again. I don't care who I have to run over, or step on in the process.

When I look up again, I notice a sign ahead. It's inside of a window, in a small brick house. It says space for rent $100 a month. It's not where I want to live, but it's a start for now, until I find out what else to do.

CHAPTER 25
Jazzy
Two Weeks Later

Cani is lying face up, on the second hand bed within the room I'm renting. Two weeks have passed since I got the room, and this is the first time I accepted a call from him. But I have my reasons, and it has nothing to do with love, or wanting to get back with him.

"Damn, baby," he says pushing into my pussy walls, as he paws my breast. "I forgot how good this shit feels." I don't speak and then he says, "Lie on the bed and spread your arms and legs." I do, and he examines my body, and then looks into my eyes. "You feel different. Where are you mentally?"

"I haven't been with anybody else, Cani," I say dryly.

"I'm not talking about physically," he says. "You don't look at me the same."

"A lot of things have happened in my life, Cani. Can we just do what you came to do?"

He gets up and walks toward the door. "Jazzy, what's going on with you? Why are you so cold these days?" he frowns at me. "Did I do something wrong?"

Cani doesn't know that I'm aware about him fucking Starr. Besides, I don't feel like him begging me for hours, trying to tell me that he didn't love her. I'm done

186

with him, and there is no turning back. Not only did he fuck my next-door neighbor, but everybody in my apartment but me knew about it. Probably the building too. I looked like a fool in front of them, and I can't get over the embarrassment.

"Cani, let's just make love," I tell him with a fake smile. "Stop faking, and get over here."

He moves toward me, and I grab at his dick to put it into my mouth. "Jazzy, what are you doing?"

I don't answer, because I'm running my tongue up and down his thickness, trying to get him to cum sooner than later. So he can just leave.

"Jazzy, I didn't wash it yet, what are you doing? I thought you didn't like to make love like this."

"I'm making you feel good. What's the problem?"

He pushes me away and I fall onto the bed. "What the fuck is this shit about," he asks frowning at me. "We never had this type of sex before without a fight. Can you stop being fake and just keep it real with me? Please?"

"Well things have changed now. I'm different, Cani."

I guess he doesn't like what I have to say, because he walks toward his clothes. Normally I would be begging him not to leave me, but I don't care anymore. When he's completely dressed he stands at the door. "You not even gonna try to make me stay? You not even going to try to talk me out of leaving?"

"If you want to leave, I can't stop you." He's about to walk out until I say, "You still gonna do that for me right?"

He looks at the floor and shakes his head. Then he stuffs his hand into his pocket, pulls out his wallet and throws one hundred dollars on the dresser. It's funny, that's more money than he ever gave me at one time when we were together. It's amazing how great men treat you when you don't give a fuck about them anymore.

"I love you, Jazzy, but I can't make you want me anymore. I don't know who has been telling lies to you about me, but the least you could do was ask me is it true before believing them. I deserve that much."

"Cani, when you leave out of the door, take that frown off of your face. You know this place only has one bedroom and the living room. Nandi is out there watching TV and I don't want her to think that we've been in here fighting. Nandi can be a handful if she thinks somebody is doing me wrong."

"Yeah...whatever."

He storms out of the room, and then leaves out the front door, without saying anything to Nandi who is sitting on the sofa. I sit next to her, and look at the TV she's watching. She's changed too over the course of us being in here, but I wonder if she's been that way all along, and we never took notice.

"How much he give you this time," she asks me, never taking her eyes off of the TV.

"One hundred dollars."

She shakes her head. "I can't believe I use to like him so much. He seems so pathetic now. Want me to take care of him?"

"No, I want you to get well." I have to do something about her. She's getting more ridiculous by the hour.

When my cell phone dings, indicating I have a new message, I pick it up. It's Kaitlin.

I don't know if anybody told U, but I found out that Aphrodite is pregnant. And, I also heard that Killion has been looking for U, bcuz of something she said. She's on the run too and nobody has been able to find her. B careful. I love you.

Now what the fuck is going on? I'm not in Killion's apartment anymore, so what the fuck does he want with me? I'm about to respond to the text when there is a knock at the door.

"You want me to get it," Nandi says.

"Naw, I got it."

I'm thinking Cani has returned either to beg me for forgiveness, or to take his money back. But when I open the door, and see it's my sister Love and Loop instead, I feel a deep hate brew inside of me.

CHAPTER 26
Love

I'm sitting on the porch of the house where Jazzy rents her room. Loop is with me, and we are both waiting for the verdict. Will she give us a few bucks to try to find a job or not? It will be really messed up if Jazzy won't let us stay a few nights with her, like we asked. We don't take up much space and I know she got the room. Spring should be coming soon, but it's been as cold as any other winter's day lately, and I don't feel safe staying in the basement of Killion's building anymore, especially after what he did to me. I hate being homeless.

"What you think she gonna do," Loop asks me.

"I don't know," I shrug. "We gotta wait and see I guess." I remember the stack of money he had when he was trying to get me to move back in the day. I never found out where he got it from. "What's up with that job you had, the one that got you all of that money that time? You can't work there again?"

"What job," he frowns, rubbing his arms so hard I think the skin is gonna slide off, and fall to the concrete. "I ain't had a job in years."

"Then where you get that money from? You never told me before. Remember, you were gonna use it to get us an apartment."

He stands up, walks to the curb, and then turns around to look at me. "Damn it, Love, this ain't what we here about. I had the money and now it's gone. We smoked half up and the other half we got robbed for, remember? Had you not forced me back on this dope shit, I wouldn't be in this situation now. So back the fuck off before I blow on you!"

I stand up, jog down the two steps and approach him. "Me," I say pointing at myself. "How you blaming me for this shit?"

"Yes you," he yells. "I was happy, Love. I didn't need this life anymore. I was clean, and was getting my life in order. Now you got me out here begging for change from the one bitch who hates me the most in the world...Jazzy! She ain't giving us no money, Love. She don't fuck with us like that."

When he says that the door opens and my sister comes outside. She's dressed in her one-piece black sweater dress, and she doesn't seem happy with me.

"Love, you're gonna need to stay with me for a couple of days," Jazzy says seriously. "Something is going down, and I'm worried about you."

I want to stay but I want Loop to be with me. "Stay with you for what," I ask. "I'm good."

"Aphrodite got pregnant, and she told Killion how she came upon her pregnancy, and I have a feeling he's going to come around looking for me. Since I don't know what else she told him, I'm worried about you too. After all, you did try to get the shot from him behind my back." My eyes widen because I'm surprised she knows.

"Yeah, I heard about what you did to me, and you know what, I still love you."

"We don't have nothing to hide," Loop says. "If Killion wants to see us, so be it."

Jazzy looks at him, and walks down the stairs. She's up in his face and I can feel my blood thicken. "I'm not talking about you, nigga. I want you as far away from my sister as possible."

"I already told you that I'm grown, Jazzy," I say to her. "Now are you gonna give me some money to help me out or not?"

"Did you know that this nigga is gay," she says pointing at Loop. "One day he was out bragging about his washed up NBA career. He came into the building so I decided to follow him, and when I did, I saw him fucking Big Titty Tina from our block. The real kicker is, Loop and I both know that Tina is a man. Isn't she Loop?"

Loop's eyes widen. "W-what are you talking about," he says trying to laugh it off. "You willing to go this far to break us up? Well I won't let that happen. Let's get out of here, Love. Your sister is tripping."

"I'm not done, tell my sister how you fucked Killion, and he gave you some money recently. From what I'm told it was a few thousand. Do you remember that, Love?" I nod yes. "Well how would I know that? It ain't like you gave me none of that money, even though we needed it badly for rent." She seems mad about that part.

Loop grabs my hand and tries to walk me away from the house, but I don't budge. I can't move. My stomach juices are splashing around inside of my body, and I feel light headed. I knew he could've gotten the money from someone who liked him, but I never thought it would be from another man. I sit on the step and look out ahead of me. "Is it true," I ask him. "Are you…I mean did you—"

Loop walks up toward me and grabs my hands. The callouses on his fingers brush against my knuckles. Suddenly I realize how much I love him, until I imagine him being with another man. Is he fucking him…sucking him…kissing him or what? Is the dude ripping his asshole out? And why does another man even turn him on? Sweat puddles on my face.

"Listen, baby, I'm not gay," he says to me. I'm immediately relieved. I knew Jazz was lying. "But sometimes you gotta do stuff that you don't want to do for money." My heart thumps. "I wanted us to get our own place, and was willing to do anything. It was only one time that I got with a man, and it didn't happen again. It didn't mean anything to me."

"That's why you wanted me out of the club that night," I say to him. "You didn't want me meeting Killion, and finding out about you."

"Baby, I didn't want you to play yourself like that. That's all. You're not a whore. Like your sister who is over here pretending to be some type of upscale kitten! When for real she's a chicken."

"You called him that night when I was at his house didn't you? The night he beat me?"

"I love you, baby. It's all I can say."

I rush over to a patch of brown bushes, and throw up into the dry leaves. I place my hand against the cold brick wall and give up everything in my stomach to the ground. When I'm done, I feel his hand on my shoulder, and I knock it off and hit him in the face with a closed fist. My hand hurts badly.

"Stay the fuck away from me," I yell. I move toward my sister who is on the step, with a sad look in her eyes. "I never want to see you again. I mean it this time."

"Love, please don't leave me," Loop says, dropping to his knees and grabbing at my ankles. "If you give up on me I'm done for. You know that shit."

"It's over!" I kick him in the face and run to the top of the stairs. Before going inside I look at him once more. "I loved you, with everything I had. I knew you weren't about shit, but I didn't care, because at least you loved me back. Even when you were addicted to heroin, I came down to that laundry room everyday, because you were mine, and I knew you needed me. I was never needed like I was when I was with you, and that meant something to me. But now," I say shaking my head, "now you ain't nothing I recognize. This is the one thing I can't deal with."

He's about to run up the stairs toward me, until Jazzy steps in front of me, blocking his path. "Don't ever come around here again, Loop. You heard her, she's done with you."

"This is all your fault," he yells, as tears stream down his face. "You couldn't let us have the kind of love we were capable of, just because of your situation with Cani. It may not be a traditional love, but we loved all the same."

"You being a faggy don't have shit to do with me and Cani. Now you heard her with your own ears, you're out of her life, and you better never come around here again."

He backs up, looks at me, and then at Jazzy. "You gonna regret this, watch. You gonna regret taking her from me, and it's gonna be real soon too."

I'm sitting on the sofa, in the living room portion of Jazzy's apartment. Nandi is next to me, and she seems extra sedated. I never saw her like this before, except for the day after Angela was murdered. She was so hysterical, that nobody could calm her down. So the doctor saw it fit to give her a light-sedative, that put her out for two days straight. I think Jazzy must have done the same thing now.

"Here's your tea," Jazzy says sitting in the middle of me and Nandi. "I put a little Hennessey in it so you can relax some."

I take the warm red mug and say, "Thank you." I look over her legs, and at Nandi who is sleeping. "What is going on with her? She looks higher than I have ever been on dope." I sip my tea.

Jazzy looks back at Nandi and then at me. "She's doing the same things again, Love. I had to up her dosages. I didn't want to, but I didn't have a choice either."

I frown. "Well what did she do?"

She explained to me how she killed Starr, tried to kill Loop on the top of the stairs with the roses, and how she killed mama. When she's done I'm more exhausted than I have ever been in my life.

I sit the cup down. "I always thought she was mentally sick because of what Cyrus did to us. But, I never knew that it was something she was born with." I shake my head softly, thinking about Loop's career in basketball, and how Nandi stole it from him, simply because she was mad. "She hurt Loop?"

"Yes, but you can't blame her."

But I do. "I don't understand, Jazzy, we aren't like her, so I wonder why she is." I could've had it all, and Love stole it from me.

"Nandi's the youngest. And you know ma was fucking with heroin heavy when she was pregnant with her. It could've been something that happened then."

When her cell phone rings I look over at her while she answers it. She picks it up and sighs. "Yes, Cani."

She looks up into the ceiling, and seems frustrated. I can tell immediately that she's done with him, and I hope the same thing will happen with my feelings toward Loop, even though I miss him terribly already.

"What...are you sure," Jazzy says as she covers her mouth. Jazzy drops the phone out of her hand, and it falls to the floor.

"What is it," I ask standing up.

"It's Bernard. He was hung from the side of our old apartment building by his neck...with a rope."

I remember Bernard. He use to live with us before Cani moved in, and I remember loving his cheerful attitude, and great food. Him having to move out is another reason I hated Cani so much, because things changed when Cani was around. I didn't get to know Bernard for a long time, but he was easy to love for the time that I did. "But why?"

"Killion did it. Aphrodite told him how she got pregnant, and he's coming for us next. We have to get out of town now!"

by Candee

CHAPTER 27
Jazzy

Everything that was worth taking was at the door. Cani let me use his truck to move my sisters to a hotel in Virginia. Although Killion didn't know where I lived, I couldn't risk him finding out either.

"Nandi is in the truck already waiting to go," Love says to me bringing a bag full of her medicines to the front. "You got everything else?"

"Yes, we good."

"I think I should double check," Love says to me.

"We don't have time, we really should be leaving now. I don't feel safe here."

We grab the rest of the bags, close and lock the door and make it to the truck. I get in the driver's seat and Nandi and Love are in the back, since I have a lot of bags in the driver's seat. It was bad packing on Love's part, but I didn't care, because I wanted us out and safe.

As I pull away from the parking lot, Nandi wakes up from a deep sleep. "What's going on, Jazzy?" she looks around. "Where are we going?"

Ever since I found out she had been killing again, I kept something powdery and white in her cup at all times. When she had juice, I laced her drink with sleeping medicine. When she ate eggs, I laced her food. I even found a way to lace her toothpaste. I needed Nandi

198

unconscious and harmless, until I discovered a way to prevent her from taking lives, simply because she could.

"We are on our way to our new place," I tell her. "Go back to sleep. I'll wake you up when we get there."

She doesn't waste any time dosing back off. When she's snoring Love asks me, "So why didn't you tell me?"

"Tell you what?" I pull up to a light and stop.

"That Loop was fucking men. You're my sister, and if you really cared about me, you would have told me. Instead you wait until the last minute to say something. I could've been infected with HIV or something."

I sigh. Love is so frustrating at times. Just draining. So what I didn't tell her he was fucking men? If I had, I still believe she would have dealt with him anyway. Even though I was surprised as anybody when Loop came over last night banging on the door, begging her back, and she wouldn't let him in. Still, I know he had her heart. And as far as her getting HIV, she could get the shit now just by sharing needles with him so I don't even want to hear that shit.

"Love, you knew about Cani fucking Starr, so why didn't you tell me?"

"Because you knew already. I can tell by the way you looked at her when she was leaving out of her apartment. Now answer my question, why didn't you tell me about Loop being gay? Do you care about me?"

"I do care about you. But, I also know what love can do to you, and I didn't think you were ready to hear the truth. If I'm wrong for that, I apologize. But we are sisters, and it's time to move past it to get our lives back on track, and our family back together."

"You were wrong, Jazzy, really wrong."

I shake my head. I don't have time for this shit, and all I want is to get them away safe. And if she wants to have a conversation with me after that, so be it.

I make a left into some residential development when I see bumper-to-bumper traffic ahead of me. I know a shortcut I never got to use before and I'm hoping it will work for us now. When I see a black Tahoe behind me, with windows so dark you can't see inside, my heart rate speeds up.

Suddenly I think about the way Loop left. He seemed angry with me and made threats I know he was sure to follow through on. "Did you talk to Loop," I ask my sister, although my eyes are still on the truck. "Before we left?"

"No. I broke up with him remember?"

"Do you think he would tell Killion where we were," I continue. "I mean is he capable of being that mean, even though it could hurt you too?"

"I don't know, Jazzy. He once told me to never underestimate the mind of a determined man. Why you ask?"

The rhythm in my heart doesn't slow down as the truck slides along my side. When all of the windows roll down, revealing a deeper blackness inside, I know our lives are over. Suddenly three shotgun barrels point in our direction, and glass particles from my window come flying inside like snowflakes on a blizzard day.

Trying to save us, I stomp my foot on the gas and press forward, but the truck maintains its position on my right side, and clips my side view mirror. I zig and zag up the road ahead of me, so that the truck can't ride next to me, but still I can't shake them.

What I see in the rear view mirror next both breaks my heart, and makes me realize that I will have nothing else to do with Love again, if we make it out of this alive. She is holding Nandi's body in front of her, to protect herself, as bullets continue to pound our truck. I can see blood gushing out of Nandi's body, as bullets strike her. I know what's about to happen now. We are going to meet Angela in heaven.

I'm so busy looking at Nandi and feeling betrayed, that I don't see the apartment building I'm about to crash into that's ahead of me. When I finally make impact, I'm flown violently forward, and then backwards. Before I know it I'm in the backseat, and my head knocks against Love's, and I'm out cold.

The moment I wake up I'm in a hospital bed with needles stuck into the pit of my arms. I snatch them out, and they sting. I have to find Nandi, to make sure she's okay. So I hop up and walk toward the entrance leading to my room. I can't believe Loop would go through so much trouble to hurt us. He didn't even care that his own girlfriend was in the car, and she could've gotten killed too. I hate him more than I ever knew was possible.

"Ma'am, what are you doing," a nurse says to me, as I look in room after room for Nandi.

"I'm looking for my sister, Nandi Law. Is she okay? Do you know where she is? I need to know she's fine."

"Ma'am, you shouldn't be moving around. You were in an accident, and the car was totaled. You lost a lot of blood, and could pass out at any time. Please go back to your room."

"I need to know where my sister is first," I scream, as my head throbs and places I didn't know was injured, burn on my body. "Fuck passing out, I want to know where she is."

Before I could dispute anymore, two men in light blue uniforms grab me. They pull me back to my room, and I'm restrained to the bed by brown leather straps on my wrists. "What the fuck is going on," I scream and kick. "Why am I being locked to the bed? I'm a victim." I feel weak.

"Ma'am, you are being restrained for your own good," a man says entering the room. I can tell he is the doctor by how high he holds his head. He's black, probably in his forties and serious. "Now my name is Dr. Curtis, and I'm in charge of your well being. You should know that I take that job seriously."

"Where is my sister," I repeat. "Nandi Law? Is she okay?"

"Yes she is, although she broke her back, and may never walk again."

I can't believe what he is saying to me, and the room feels like it's spinning. Why is all of this happening? "What...do you mean? Is she paralyzed?"

"I'm afraid so," he says. "From the waist down."

Although the hate I feel for Love is heavy, I still want to know about her too. "Well what about my other sister? Love Law?"

He looks at the other nurses in the room, and they all shake their heads. "We don't know of any other person involved in your accident. The only person at the scene was Nandi, and she suffered bullet wounds to the spine. And we will need her to stay here, so we can monitor her before she is released."

"Someone did leave you this letter though," one of the male nurses says, placing a folded sheet of paper in my hand. He realized I couldn't open the paper in the restraints, so he took the letter, opened it and placed it back in my hand.

When I look at the bottom and see Love's name I say, "Can I be alone?"

"Sure," the doctor says. "But try to take it easy. Remember, you lost a lot of blood and will need your rest, Ms. Law. You can't operate mentally and physically like you did before the accident. I just want to make that clear. When I am sure you are okay, I will remove the restraints."

"I understand," I say. I just want them gone.

When they finally leave I start my letter.

Dear Jazzy,

I was disappointed when I called to check on your status today, and found out you were still alive. I went through so much to see to it that you finally

got what you deserved, and once again you proved to be smarter than me.

I'm not going to lie, I wanted to believe the fairytale that me, you and Nandi could all live happily ever after, but I'm not a child anymore. I could never live with you again because I don't love you. I don't even like you.

You knew how much I loved Loop, and still you couldn't let me have him. So what did you do, tell me that evil story just so I would let him go. Well it didn't work, because we are in love and back together.

In case you blame Loop for this whole ordeal with the car accident, don't. It was me who called Killion to tell him where you lived. I did it just before we left, and I had hoped to stall long enough so that he could kill you at home, but you were too busy rushing. I hated to use Nandi's body to protect my own, but she's crazy and deserves to die for what she did to Loop too.

Don't worry though; I'll let Killion know where you are now. You'll be surprised how much he pays for this type of information. He even forgave me for the supposed robbery.

Your Ex-Sister, Love

When I'm done, I put the letter down and cry all over the page. I did all I could for Love, and I don't have any more compassion in my heart for her. She's dead to me, and I mean that more now than ever.

I look down at the restraints on my arm and sigh. I can't do anything to defend me or Nandi if Killion comes blasting through this hospital. I'm at a loss and I don't know what to do. I think I don't have any other options until Cani walks through the door.

"Oh, you're up," he says. "I just came from seeing Nandi. Jazz I'm so sorry about all of this shit," he sits the roses on the table. "How do you feel?"

"I'm fine, how is she?"

"She looks tired, but I sang to her and put a smile on that face. I wish I could do something just as simple for you, but I know it won't work. How are you?"

"Are you sure she's fine," I ask ignoring everything else.

"She is, baby. Don't worry about her, I made sure she was fine before I left." He looks down at my arm. "Why are you restrained?"

"Because I was going to see about Nandi, and they didn't want me to get out of bed."

"You know you need to be resting. My truck was totaled, and the accident was bad. I can only imagine what's going on in your body right now."

"I don't have time for that shit. Killion may be on his way right now to finish what he started." I tell him about the letter Love sent me, and everything she had in it. "So you see, Cani, I need you to do something for me."

"What is it, baby?"

"I need you to reach out to Killion."

He chuckles. "Yeah right, that faggy not gonna let me get within five feet of him. If he's smart anyway, especially after what he did to you."

"He will if you go at him how I tell you too."

CHAPTER 28
Jazzy
(One Week Later)

I'm in the kitchen preparing a ham and cheese sandwich for Nandi. After leaving the hospital, Cani helped me get a place in Maryland, far away from where I use to live. Although he comes over periodically, I made it clear that I need to be alone to figure out what I want to do with my life. A relationship was the last thing on my mind, and for now he seems to understand. To this day I'm still looking for Aphrodite, who owes me money.

When I'm done making Nandi's lunch, I grab her orange juice and the keys off of the table. Once I'm at her door, I unlock it and go inside. I sit the sandwich on the small table inside her room, and stand at the door-way.

Nandi is still on her bed, with her back faced in my direction. I don't know if she's up or not, because she isn't moving. "Hello, Nandi, how do you feel," I ask softly.

"Fine," she mumbles.

I swallow and take one more step inside. "I brought your sandwich, did you want to eat it now or later."

"Now is fine. Can you help me up please?"

I walk deeper into her room, grab her wheel chair and push it toward the bed. She lifts her upper body, and I wrap my arms around her, helping her into the chair. For a second she holds too tightly onto me, but she eventually lets me go. Sometimes Nandi scares me and I never know how to take her.

Once she's in her chair, I push her towards the table. She picks up the sandwich, bites down into it and looks at me. "Thank you," she says with her mouth full. "Can you leave me alone now?"

"Nandi, are you angry with me for something?"

"Why do you have to lock me in here, like I'm some sort of animal? That's not right, Jazzy. I'm your sister, and I have feelings."

"I lock you in here because I'm worried. I'm worried about what you're capable of and what you might do to people. But you know I love you, Nandi."

"In case you haven't looked at me in a while, I can't walk." She throws the half eaten sandwich on the table. "How can I get out of here to hurt anyone, Jazzy? Are you at least thinking about what you're saying, before you say it? I was shot five times, and then I come home to be treated like this. It's not fair. I feel like I'm in prison."

"I'm sorry, I just can't let you out right now."

I back out of the room, close the door, and use the keys to lock it shut. I hear a small thud on the door, and figure she threw her sandwich like she had many times since our arrangement. I know it's probably wrong, but I can't trust her, and since I can't trust her, I can't let her out. I even gave her the master bedroom, with the bathroom attached, so she'll have everything she needs. I use to sedate her heavily, but her liver took a hit, and I had to back off. For now locking her in the room, is my only solution.

When I hear a knock at the door, I look out of the peephole. It's Cani, but before I open it I go to the living room window, and look outside to be sure he's alone. I know he won't hurt me, but Killion is still trying to find me and my sister, and I need to take all precautions.

When the coast is clear, I let him inside. "Hey, beautiful," he says kissing me on my cheek because I turn my head. "Wow, after everything I did you still don't love me huh?"

"Cani, you cheated on me behind my back. And then my sisters found out but nobody told me. You don't realize how dumb that makes me feel. I trusted you with everything, and that shit was in vain. As far as you taking care of me, I took care of you for years without question. So you owe me."

He pulls me to his body, and I allow him to hold me for a second because he's paying the rent. "I'm sorry, Jazzy, you know I am. And if you give me some time I'm gonna show you how much I love you. I'll do anything, just say the word."

"I told you what you can do if you really want me back."

He walks away, leaving me alone. "I can't do that shit." He sits on the sofa, turns the TV on and crosses his feet over my glass table. "As much as I care about you, doing what you're asking me is out of the question. It goes against everything I believe."

"This nigga is trying to kill me, Cani. You saw what he did to your truck. He's not going to stop until he finishes me and Nandi off. Now you say you love me, and all I'm asking you to do is lure him to the motel. You're so attractive he will take the bait the moment he sees your face, I promise you. And when he does, you just call me and I'll come and take care of him myself."

"You don't even have a gun, Jazz. What are you talking about?"

I walk in front of him, and remove the nine I got from Kaitlin from my waist, that I keep with me. I aim it at him and he ducks. For a fleeting moment I think about accidently shooting him, for breaking my heart, but the gun doesn't belong to me. I put it down.

"You gotta be careful with them things, Jazz. You could've shot me. That's why you don't need it, you don't know what you're doing."

"So as you can see I got a gun," I say ignoring him. "Now what? Are you going to help me or not? Please, Cani."

He sighs. "It ain't in me to lure another nigga to a motel off the pretense of fucking him. It just ain't my style."

"You got a lot of excuses for a nigga who claims he wants a bitch back." He rolls his eyes and I can tell I'm breaking him, so I walk over to the sofa and sit on his lap. "Cani, do this for me. Please. Lure him to the motel and I'll do the rest. I promise you, that you will not regret this. Are you gonna do it for me or not? I'm begging you."

CHAPTER 29
Cani

The red and green club lights bounced off of Cani's lavender shirt. He left three of the buttons unfastened at the top, so that the soft hair lying against his chest was visible. Although the shirt covered his upper body, it was tight enough to tell he was in shape, without trying too hard. He was definitely soft on the eyes, and a gorgeous man to look at. The base booming from the speaker behind him made him feel stronger, and he hoped it would last long enough for what he had to do.

Killion was in the VIP section as usual, with five men around him, and double that amount in females. They were dressed in colorful outfits, and the smiles on their faces showed everyone that they were having a good time.

Cani had been eyeing Killion the entire night, and at first he thought he was lucky enough not to be his type, until there was a pathway on the dance floor, and Killion could see him clearly. Before Cani knew it, Killion was whispering into the female's ear, who was wearing a pink tight dress. She took one look at Cani, smiled and wiggled over into his direction.

The pretty girl placed her hand on Cani's shoulder, and pulled down lightly so she could whisper into his ear. "My friend wants me to ask if he knows you from somewhere." Her minty breath tickled his nose. "He says you look familiar."

Cani looked over at Killion and said, "Tell him he knows me from high school." He figured if Killion was gay, he would keep the lie alive.

She smiled. "He thought so. He wants to invite you over for drinks, that is if you have time." He nodded yes. "Great, so what's your name again?"

"Bravo."

"Cool name, Bravo. Follow me."

Killion walked over to the VIP with the pretty girl who was holding his hand. When they made it to the private section, the pretty girl whispered into his ear. After that Killion introduced Cani to everyone as his old high school friend, who he hadn't seen in years. He was officially a homo and Cani hated him. But the dude in a red jacket, who moved everywhere Killion went, didn't seem to like Cani.

Cani had been over there for an hour, and had drink after drink with the ladies. For a second he forgot Killion was the enemy, because he was having such a good time. He danced with the girl wearing the pink dress, and even danced with the young lady in red. When a pretty waitress bought over five more bottles of Ace of Spades', and three bottles of Ciroc in regular, peach and berry flavors, things were kicked up to another level.

"Everybody dig in," Killion said, stealing one last look at Cani.

Cani patiently waited for everyone else to refresh their cups, and when they were done, he moved to grab the regular Ciroc, until the man who had been eyeing him all night snatched the bottle away.

"The name is Lewis, and I don't remember you from school."

"So, that ain't my problem," Cani said reaching for the bottle again.

"Ain't no more for you. You cut off from the drinks, until you keep shit real."

"Fuck you mean ain't no more for me?"

"You heard me," he said, not backing down. "I know all of Killion's friends from high school, and I don't remember you."

"Maybe you don't know as many people as you thought you did."

"What's up with you," he persisted. "What do you really want with Killion?"

"You know what, let me go rap to my man right quick, and I'm out of here. I don't have time for this shit." Cani walked over to Killion. He was talking to two women so he said, "Excuse me ladies. I got to rap to him right quick." When they were gone Cani spoke in a low voice that only Killion could hear. "I'm getting ready to bounce. Your boy over there is about to make me rise on him. If you want to get your dick sucked tonight, meet me at this address." He handed him the folded piece of paper he prepared earlier, before coming to the club. "I'm from out of town and I'm only gonna be there tonight. Hopefully I'll see you before I leave."

Cani walked away without checking Killion's facial expressions. Saying those words was the hardest thing *he had to do in his life, but now it was over. He took it for the Team...Team Jazzy.*

When he made it out of the club, he walked past a group of girls and winked. When he was away from them, he moved toward the side of the building, away from the crowd, and vomited. Replaying what he had to say to another man over and over in his mind fucked with his head. Made him feel emasculated. But, for the return of Jazzy's love, he was prepared to do anything. He only hoped it was worth it.

CHAPTER 30
Cani

Two hours passed since Cani gave Killion the invitation to the motel. He paced the floor from the window to the bed so many times, it was amazing that the brown rug wasn't rubbed off. He called Jazzy twenty times to get a hold of her, and to tell her that he was there, but his calls went unanswered so he decided to leave a voicemail instead.

Jazz, where you at? I'm at the motel waiting on this nigga, but you not here. Hurry up.

After three hours, Killion's black Maybach pulled up in front of the motel. Cani stepped away from the window, took a few deep breaths, and walked over to the table to set up his video camera on his iPhone. He hid it behind the coffee machine and cups, so it couldn't be seen with the naked eye. Since Jazzy wouldn't answer the phone, he wanted proof for her that he actually showed up, and did what she asked him too, before he bounced.

Killion knocked on the door three quick times and Cani opened it. "What up, man," Cani responded, giving him a one arm handshake like most men do. He closed the door. "I was about to roll out. I thought you got held up."

Killion didn't respond. Instead he walked into the room and inspected the bathroom and closet. Cani's heart rocked believing in any second, he would see the phone he had set up that was recording everything he did.

"Everything cool," Cani asked, trying to break his examination, before he found the phone.

"Yeah." Killion approached him, forcing Cani to back up against the door. "So where you wanna do it?"

"Do what?"

Killion pulled his pants down, and the belt buckle that slammed against the floor sounded like thunder in Cani's ear. "You said you were gonna suck my dick, so where you wanna do it?"

Cani walked around him. "Wait a minute, man." He tried to chuckle to hide his horror, but it came out high pitched and low, like a female's. "You just got here. I figured we could grab some drinks first, and get to know each other. Why you coming at me all hard and shit?"

Killion approached him, and pushed Cani's shoulder downward, so that his butt slammed against the edge of the bed. Then he grabbed his dick, and tried to go toward Cani's mouth. Cani jumped up, pushed him back and said, "Listen, ain't nothing wrong with us having a good time, but you coming at me sideways. Slow down, homeboy."

"You not gay are you," Killion frowned, pants still at his ankles. "You be with that bitch, the one I'm looking for, named Jazzy."

Cani remained quiet.

Upscale KITTENS

"You think I'm dumb," Killion laughed. "Nigga, her sister Love told me everything about ya'll. I knew who you were the moment I saw you come into the club. To be honest, we had plans to kill you and dump you out back tonight, but you got mad and left early."

"How you know I wasn't strapped?"

"My girls frisked you when they were dancing with you. And I had somebody on this motel the moment you gave me the address, so I knew you were alone. When you said you would hook me up in the motel, I figured I would see how far you were willing to go to save your friend's life." Killion brandished a gun and aimed it at Cani. "So let me ask you now, how far are you willing to go?"

Cani was horrified. He didn't know what could happen when he agreed to meet him at the motel, but he never suspected this. So he threw his hands up in the air. "Listen, man, I meant everything I said in the club, and I don't know nothing about no chick name Love. If you would just—" Cani cut his own statement off after he charged Killion, by ramming his upper body into his waist. He wanted to catch him off guard, and take the gun.

Killion's body slammed against the TV, and Cani hit him with a firm right to the fleshy part of his cheek. The gun fell from his hand and landed at the foot of the bed. Killion couldn't get his bearings together, due to his pants being at his ankles, so he threw a few gut punches at Cani. Cani balled over momentarily, due to the force of his blows, but he got himself together quickly to fight back.

217

by Candee

The room was becoming a crime scene as blood splashed everywhere. Physically fit, and a light drinker, allowed Cani to get the best of Killion. That is until Killion hit Cani over the head with a wooden table top, that once held the TV up. Cani fell to the floor, and from his view he could see Killion pulling his pants up and then going for the gun.

When Killion wiggled for the gun by the bed, Cani grabbed his ankle, bringing his body falling down over his head. Using all of his strength, Cani covered his stomach with the gun, and tried his best to get it. Only God knew who would reign supreme.

When Cani rolled over, and two shots sounded off, Killion's body slid off of him, and fell at the foot of the bed. Cani jumped up with the gun in hand and paced the floor. He just committed murder.

"Oh my, God, what the fuck have I done," he yelled. "What the fuck have I done?" Cani quickly rushed for the motel's phone, preparing to call the police. But when he saw the door crashing in with ten cops, who all had guns aimed in his direction, he knew all was lost.

Epilogue

Aphrodite was lying on her side, with tears crawling down her face. In the hospital bed after just giving birth, she was having post partum depression of the worst kind.

It had been six months since Cani Rodriquez murdered Killion Holmes, and only God knew why. Her plan to convince Killion that she could be the perfect woman for him blew up in her face, after the news of his death. The only blessing was her precious baby girl name Anna Bell, who at two days old was the heir to Killion's throne.

Aphrodite was preparing to cry some more, until the door opened and the nurse pushing a cart full of pills strolled inside. "I don't want anything else. I feel loopy already."

The nurse didn't appear to be listening, as she pushed the cart until it rammed against the side of the bed. Aphrodite was preparing to yell at her, until Jazzy raised her head, and revealed her face. She pointed a gun in her direction, silencing her immediately. "I'm gonna be quick, because time is not on our side. You owe me, and I want my payout."

"Uh, Jazzy, uh—"

"Before you say anything let me show you something." Jazzy sat on the edge of her bed, pulled out her cell phone, and handed it to Aphrodite.

Aphrodite covered her mouth and sobbed heavily into her hand. "Oh my, God, please tell me you don't have my baby."

"I don't, but my sister does." Jazzy said. "And I don't know if I told you or not, but my sister is in a wheel chair, angry and crazy. The quicker we get the baby back the better."

Aphrodite eyed the picture of a baby covered in a blanket in Nandi's lap, while she sat in the wheel chair. When she had it too long, Jazzy snatched the phone away from her.

"What do you want from me? Please don't hurt my baby," she sobbed.

When a nurse walked by and stuck her head in the door she said, "Mrs. Governor are you okay?"

Aphrodite looked at Jazzy. She was contemplating telling her to go get the police. Perhaps if she went right now, Jazzy would be arrested and her baby would be returned to her before the night visited. But what if the move backfired in her face, she would never see her child again. And she would never be able to deal with herself.

"Uh...yes...I'm fine."

"That's great. Would you like me to—,"

"Get out," Aphrodite yelled, cutting her off. "Please!"

The nurse frowned. "As you wish." She walked away.

"That was smart, real smart," Jazzy commended her.

"Fuck you, bitch," Aphrodite yelled and spit at the same time. *"Now stop fucking around with me, and tell me what I got to do to get my baby back."*

"Now you're a businesswoman." Jazzy laughed. *"For starters you are going to transfer fifty thousand dollars to my banking account right now."*

"Done," Aphrodite explained.

"Not done until you do it. You burned me once, but you not gonna do it again." Jazzy threw her iPad into Aphrodite's lap, which was already queued up and ready to go.

Aphrodite looked at her bank account's logo on the screen. *"How did you know where I banked?"*

"I been following you for months, Aphrodite." She looked at the open doorway. *"Now hurry the fuck up. I'm in a hurry."*

"You had something to do with Killion's murder too, didn't you?"

"Of course, although I must tell you it wasn't easy. But, I know if Cani doesn't like one thing in the world, it's a gay man. I was sure that if I left him alone with him long enough, that he would do exactly what happened, commit murder, and send Killion's evil ass to hell." Jazzy smiled and said, *"Now stop fucking around and transfer my money."*

Aphrodite tapped the screen on Jazzy's iPad harder than what was necessary, but when Jazzy saw the green success sign flash, she didn't care. The money was officially hers. Aphrodite pushed the iPad back to her when *she was done. "Now you got your money, where is my baby?"*

"Not yet, because as I see it, you owe me your undying attention and money. Had it not been for me, you would not be the custodian over your child's estate. That's a million dollar baby I helped you get, so in a sense we're partners. So, you will drop this amount of money in my account every month. Now since you're a millionaire I know you can do more, but that will do good for now. Besides, I have plans to earn my keep. I've started a little organization that will help me get on my feet, and all I need you to do is fund it."

"What makes you think I will do that," she asked swiping the tears away from her face.

"Because I will tell everyone how you and I spent time together going over a plan to trap Killion into a pregnancy. You don't know it, but one of Nandi's many talents, outside of babysitting, is snapping pictures." Jazzy showed her the photo on the phone of she, the late Bernard and Aphrodite at the table, at her house, drinking wine. "With this kind of proof, and considering Bernard's fate they won't have a problem believing me Especially if I tell them you killed Killion to take his estate."

"You are so wrong. I can't believe—"

"No, bitch, what's wrong is how you turned a debt from one thousand dollars, into one that you will pay over a lifetime, which resulted in a good man dying. All you had to do was give me $500 and keep your mouth closed, and you couldn't do either. And because of it,

you will also donate a thousand dollars a month to the LGBT community, in Bernard's name."

"Whatever, where is my baby," she yelled. She was beyond frustrated.

Jazzy stood up, and grabbed her purse. "I don't know," she shrugged. "I don't have your baby."

Without waiting to see if Jazzy was playing or not, she screamed to the top of her lungs. And instead of running, Jazzy stood in place, and waited for her fate. A doctor and the nurse who stopped by earlier, came rushing inside the room. "What's wrong, Ms. Governor, are you okay," the doctor questioned.

"My baby, my baby, where is she?"

"Go get her baby," the doctor ordered.

Jazzy stood as cool as rain, as she waited for the verdict. Within seconds, a baby dressed in a white blanket with pink hearts was brought inside. "Here she is right here. She was sleeping in her crib the entire time. I was coming to ask if you wanted me to get her so that you could breastfeed her earlier, but you yelled at me and told me to get out." Jazzy winked and walked out of the room.

Once she was inside of her old, but still pretty white Benz, she let the top down and drove to her next destination. Under the name Upscale Kittens, which she got from Loop, she was helping gold-diggers across America get pregnant, and get rich at the same time. She stopped fucking with chicken heads, and broke bitches who couldn't afford her services, and her rates skyrocketed. Jazzy demanded five thousand just to meet with a client, and fifteen thousand upon receipt of the shot. Be-

cause her services could also get her killed, she only dealt with the elite, the upscale, and they were the only ones who knew her name.

When Jazzy stopped at the intersection of Minnesota Avenue, and Benning road, Love and Loop couldn't believe their eyes when they saw her sitting in the beautiful car. They were standing outside panhandling, and looking a mess. Judging by the way the real diamonds sparkled in her ears, it was evident that she had made a come up.

"Jazzy, Jazzy," Love yelled, waving her arms. "Sister, it's me."

Jazzy turned around, took one look at Love, and rolled her eyes. Secretly her heart broke down on the inside, seeing the condition of Love's dusty skin, tattered clothing and missing teeth. She also looked at Loop, who didn't look any better. But, she made her bed and for once she would make her lie in it.

"You got the wrong person," she told her. "I got one sister and it damn sure ain't you." When the light turned green she pulled off without another word.

Jazzy was done with her, and she finally meant what she said. Besides, she had her hands full with Nandi who required around the clock care. Jazzy could deal with Nandi's mental illness, because she couldn't help herself. But Love was selfish, jealous and untrustworthy, a combination she didn't want to be associated with anymore.

Besides she was a businesswoman now with a growing operation. Jazzy spent her days meeting clients, and her nights working with Nandi. Who had time for games?

She hired a young brilliant doctor who was fresh out of school, and eager to work with Nandi. Before long the doctor found the perfect meds to balance Nandi's mental condition, and personality and Jazzy loved the headway they were making.

Jazzy even hired a physical therapist to help Nandi walk, and major progress was being made. All was right with the world, but now she had to make one more stop.

Nandi pulled up in front of the DC Jail, to take care of her last business for the day. She waited five minutes, before Cani strolled out. The sun seemed to block his view, as he looked up and down the street for his ride. When he saw the bling of Jazzy's earrings, he smiled, and walked over to the car.

Cani had the worst six months in his life, after being accused of Killion's murder. For two months he told anybody with ears that he was innocent, and how he defended himself after Killion pushed himself onto him sexually. But when he told Jazzy where to get the phone from the motel, that showed the entire crime, she hadn't bothered to return his call. For weeks he feared the worst that she had let him down. He was surprised the cops didn't check the room properly but they were sloppy as usual.

Cani had no idea that Jazzy, still bitter about him fucking Starr, thought about leaving him in prison to rot in hell. It was only after news got back to her that he was being constantly beaten, due to people assuming he was gay, that she gave in and helped him out. She fig-

ured the reputation of being gay on the DC streets, would hurt him far more than anything she could do to him.

When Cani eased into the Benz, and Jazzy saw his face, she couldn't believe her eyes. Cani's once beautiful complexion was riddled with maroon marks, and one of his teeth were missing. Them DC boys had certainly put a beating on him.

"Thank you for coming," he reached for a kiss, but she backed up toward the mirror. "I'm so happy to be free."

"I told you I was coming," she said pulling off, with an attitude.

"So where we going," he smiled, hoping the niggas who once thought he was gay, would see him with the beautiful Jazzy, and form new opinions. "I'm hungry as shit, and want some real food."

"I'm going home, but what I want to know is where am I taking you?"

He observed her, finally realizing that she changed even more. Before the murder, he knew things were different between them, but now it was evident. He could feel it! She didn't look at him with the same admiration. "I was hoping you would take me with you, Jazzy, I mean I did kill a man for you. Can you spend some time with me at least? A few hours?"

"And I got you a lawyer, and helped get you off too. Remember that shit? I even brought the video to him, showing how you fought for your life. It was because of me your case turned to self defense. That's the only rea-

son you're free right now, Cani. If anything you owe me."

"Jazzy, I love—"

"Let me stop you right there," she said throwing her car into park. "I don't love you anymore, Cani. I'm done with the love thing between us. Now I appreciate you deading that nigga for me, because he was fucking with my family, and for your troubles I got you this." She reached into her purse, and handed him a stack of one hundred dollar bills. "That's twenty thousand dollars, enough to get you some business and a new start. But take your eyes off of me because we are over, and I don't belong to you anymore."

His eyes widened as he gripped the money stack. "Are you serious?"

He was irritating so she popped the door locks. "If you gonna act like a female get out of my fucking car, I'm done with you."

"So you gonna throw me out, like I don't fucking matter? Bitch, I will kill you in this mothafucka," he yelled. "Fuck this money! You ruined my life!"

"You mean kill me and get locked up for the rest of your life," Jazzy giggled. "Come on, Cani, you not built like that. Word hit the streets about how you were taking dick in there better than the baddest bitch on the streets. Got niggas calling you Kim Kardashian and everything. You not made for no prison life, I'm telling you. Now get the fuck out, before I go to the precinct, and tell them that an ex-convict is out here threatening me."

Cani slowly got out of the car. "You gonna remember—"

by Candee

He would've liked to said, you gonna remember this shit. But Jazzy pulled off so fast, he was speaking to her bumper instead.

Oh yes, Jazzy Law changed. She was about her money and nothing else mattered. She was moving so fast, that she couldn't feel the list of enemies that she had collected along the way, but she would soon find out.

Drunk & Hot Girls

The Complete Series

By
LEGACY CARTER

CARTEL PUBLICATIONS
PRESENTS

HERSBAND
MATERIAL
A NOVEL

BY C. WASH

CARTEL PUBLICATIONS
PRESENTS

The Cartel Collection
Established in January 2008
We're growing stronger by the month!!!
www.thecartelpublications.com

Cartel Publications Order Form
Inmates ONLY get novels for $10.00 per book!

Titles		*Fee*
Shyt List		$15.00
Shyt List 2		$15.00
Pitbulls In A Skirt		$15.00
Pitbulls In A Skirt 2		$15.00
Pitbulls In A Skirt 3		$15.00
Pitbulls In A Skirt 4		$15.00
Victoria's Secret		$15.00
Poison		$15.00
Poison 2		$15.00
Hell Razor Honeys		$15.00
Hell Razor Honeys 2		$15.00
A Hustler's Son 2		$15.00
Black And Ugly As Ever		$15.00
Year of The Crack Mom		$15.00
The Face That Launched a Thousand Bullets		
		$15.00
The Unusual Suspects		$15.00
Miss Wayne & The Queens of DC		
		$15.00
Year of The Crack Mom		$15.00
Familia Divided		$15.00
Shyt List III		$15.00
Shyt List IV		$15.00
Raunchy		$15.00
Raunchy 2		$15.00
Raunchy 3		$15.00
Reversed		$15.00
Quita's Dayscare Center		$15.00
Quita's Dayscare Center 2		$15.00
Shyt List V		$15.00
Deadheads		$15.00
Pretty Kings		$15.00
Drunk & Hot Girls		$15.00
Hersband		$15.00
Upscale Kittens		$15.00

Please add $4.00 *per book* for shipping and handling.
The Cartel Publications * P.O. Box 486 * Owings Mills * MD * 21117

Name: _____

Address:_____

City/State:_____

Contact # & Email:_____

Please allow 5-7 business days for delivery. The Cartel is not
responsible for prison orders rejected.

Personal Checks Are Not Accepted.

Made in the USA
Charleston, SC
07 July 2013